MURDER
GETS A
MAKEOVER

Books by Laura Levine

THIS PEN FOR HIRE
LAST WRITES
KILLER BLONDE
SHOES TO DIE FOR
THE PMS MURDER
DEATH BY PANTYHOSE
CANDY CANE MURDER
KILLING BRIDEZILLA
KILLER CRUISE
DEATH OF A TROPHY WIFE
GINGERBREAD COOKIE MURDER
PAMPERED TO DEATH
DEATH OF A NEIGHBORHOOD WITCH
KILLING CUPID
DEATH BY TIARA
MURDER HAS NINE LIVES
DEATH OF A BACHELORETTE
DEATH OF A NEIGHBORHOOD SCROOGE
DEATH OF A GIGOLO
CHRISTMAS SWEETS
MURDER GETS A MAKEOVER

Published by Kensington Publishing Corp.

MURDER GETS A MAKEOVER

LAURA LEVINE

KENSINGTON
PUBLISHING CORP.

www.kensingtonbooks.com

KENSINGTON BOOKS are published by

Kensington Publishing Corp.
119 West 40th Street
New York, NY 10018

All Kensington Titles, Imprints, and Distributed Lines are available at special quantity discounts for bulk purchases for sales promotions, premiums, fund-raising, and educational or institutional use. Special book excerpts or customized printings can also be created to fit specific needs. For details, write or phone the office of the Kensington special sales manager: Kensington Publishing Corp., 119 West 40th Street, New York, NY 10018, attn: Special Sales Department, Phone: 1-800-221-2647.

Library of Congress Card Catalogue Number: 2021936541

The K logo is a trademark of Kensington Publishing Corp.

ISBN-13: 978-1-4967-2813-5
ISBN-10: 1-4967-2813-0
First Kensington Hardcover Edition: October 2021

ISBN-13: 978-1-4967-2815-9 (ebook)
ISBN-10: 1-4967-2815-7 (ebook)

10 9 8 7 6 5 4 3 2 1

Printed in the United States of America

For Frank Mula,
my rescuing angel

ACKNOWLEDGMENTS

As always, major thanks to my editor, John Scognamiglio, for his unwavering faith in Jaine—and for coming up with both the title and the premise of this book. Merci beaucoup, John. You're the best!

And kudos to my rock of an agent, Evan Marshall, for his much-appreciated guidance and support.

Thanks to Hiro Kimura, who so brilliantly brings Prozac to life on my book covers. To Lou Malcangi for another fantastic dust jacket design. And to the rest of the gang at Kensington who keep Jaine and Prozac coming back for murder and minced mackerel guts each year.

Special thanks to Frank Mula, treasured friend and man of a thousand jokes. To Mara and Lisa Lideks. And to Dorothy Howell, author of the very funny Haley Randolph mystery series, for her help wrangling Jaine's parents in Tampa Vistas.

To Joanne Fluke for a killer blurb. To Mark Baker for sticking with me all these years. To my friends and family for your love and encouragement. And a great big XOXO to my readers. I'm grateful for every single one of you.

Finally, a heartfelt thanks to my amazing neighbors— Barbara Engel and Richard Thompson, Lauryn Saviero-Seibert, and Laura Burckhardt (and her roomies, Jen, Rachel, and Darby). I couldn't have made it through the COVID pandemic without your extraordinary kindness and generosity. I hope by the time this book is in print, it will be safe to have you all over to my house for wine and fudge and socially un-distanced hugs!

MURDER
GETS A
MAKEOVER

Prologue

Sure, I've had my regrets:
My first (and only) bikini wax.
My first (and only) bikini.
Thinking a spin class would be fun.
Or hanging wallpaper would be easy.
Every blind date (and bathroom scale) I've ever been on.
All the naps I haven't taken.
All the chocolate I haven't eaten.

But they all pale in comparison to my disastrous decision to get a fashion makeover.

If only I'd stayed true to my elastic-waist pants and ketchup-stained sweats, I would never have wound up with a murder rap hanging over my head.

On the day it all began, I was at my computer, writing an ad for one of my biggest clients, Toiletmasters Plumbers, extolling the virtues of their double-flush commode. But it wasn't easy. Not with my cat Prozac perched on my windowsill, hissing like an asthmatic radiator.

The object of her rancor was a particularly bushy-tailed squirrel scampering up my neighbor's drainpipe. Prozac had been fixated on this critter for the past several days, going bonkers whenever she saw it.

"Prozac," I snapped, after staring at the same sentence for fifteen minutes. "Stop that hissing right now!"

Ever cooperative, she stopped hissing. And started yowling instead.

"What is it with you?" I groaned. "It's just a squirrel."

She tore her eyes away from the window just long enough to shoot me a withering glare.

Just a squirrel? Can't you see it's an evil alien from the Planet Acorn, out to destroy democracy as we know it? Only I can save the world from total doom!

What can I say? My cat's delusional. I didn't name her Prozac for nothing.

So there I was, slaving away on Toiletmasters' double-flush commode, wondering if I could trade in Prozac for a goldfish, when my neighbor Lance came knocking at my front door. I hustled him inside before Prozac had a chance to dash out and do battle with her acorn-loving nemesis.

"I've got fabulous news!" Lance gushed, sailing into my apartment in a designer suit, his blond curls moussed to perfection. "Bebe Braddock wants to give you a fashion makeover!"

"Bebe who?"

"Bebe Braddock, stylist to the stars! She dresses all the A-list Hollywood celebrities, and she's one of my most loyal customers at Neiman's."

The Neiman's to which he referred was Neiman Marcus, the famed department store, where Lance is gainfully employed as a shoe salesman, fondling the tootsies of the rich and famous.

"Bebe wants to do a 'Before & After' makeover on her Instagram page, and I convinced her to use you! I told her what a fashion disaster you were!"

"Did you now? How very thoughtful."

As usual, my sarcasm soared over his blond curls.

"No need to thank me, hon. That's what friends are for. Anyhow, I showed her a picture of you in your CUCKOO FOR COCOA PUFFS T-shirt, and she can't wait to turn you from frumpy to fabulous."

Frumpy? Who the heck was he calling frumpy?

"For your information, I happen to like the way I dress. It's California Casual."

"Only if you're dumpster diving in Malibu. Seriously, Jaine. There are vultures circling over our duplex, waiting for your clothes to die."

"Forget it. No way am I giving up my elastic-waist pants and cutting off the free flow of calories from my lips to my hips."

Lance shook his head in disgust.

"I can't believe you're passing up this golden opportunity. Isn't she crazy, Pro?"

Prozac, having abandoned her yowling to slither around Lance's ankles, purred in agreement.

I'll say. She doesn't even believe in evil aliens from the Planet Acorn.

Lance took off in a cloud of disapproval, and the minute he was gone, Prozac jumped back up on the windowsill and resumed yowling.

Seeking refuge from the din, I headed out to the supermarket to stock up on fruits and vegetables. (Okay, peanut butter and Double Stuf Oreos.)

I drove over, still steaming at Lance. The nerve of that guy. Calling me a fashion disaster.

My thoughts about Lance were put on hold, however, when I pulled into the parking lot and saw a bunch of teenagers tossing empty soda cans into the trash. How irresponsible, when there was a clearly marked bin for recyclables right next to it.

Now I happen to care about the planet almost as much

as I care about Double Stuf Oreos. So I marched over and started retrieving the cans from the trash.

Unfortunately, they were at the bottom of the bin, and I had to bend over quite a bit to reach them.

I was trying to fish them out when I felt someone tap me on the shoulder.

I turned around to see a distinguished old gent in tweeds and tasseled loafers.

"Here, my dear," he said, holding out a twenty-dollar bill. "Use this to buy yourself something to eat. And bus fare to a homeless shelter."

Good heavens! He thought I was homeless.

"No, no. You don't understand, sir. I was trying to recycle."

"This is no time for foolish pride, young lady. Just take the money and get yourself a hot meal. Maybe stop off at the Goodwill for a change of outfit, too."

I stood there, dazed, as he walked away.

Then, for the first time that day, I took a good look at my outfit.

I flushed, ashamed, when I realized I could play connect-the-dots with the ketchup stains on my sweats.

Maybe Lance was right. Maybe it was time to update my look.

So I took out my cell and called him.

"Hey, Lance," I said when he picked up. "It's me, Jaine."

And then I uttered those fateful words I'd soon live to regret:

"I think I'll try that makeover after all."

Chapter 1

A few days later, I set out from my duplex on the low-rent fringes of Beverly Hills and tootled over to Bebe's spread in the posh neighborhood of Brentwood. It was a sprawling, cottage-like affair with a gabled roof and dormer windows, and its velvety lawn was abloom with roses, hydrangeas, and peonies the size of volleyballs.

All surrounded by a quaint picket fence.

Think *Ozzie and Harriet* on steroids.

Unlatching the picket gate, I made my way up a brick pathway to the front door, past a battalion of security signs warning would-be burglars of surveillance cameras and armed guards on call.

Awash in the scent of freshly mowed grass and newly minted money, I rang the bell, and seconds later, the door swung open to reveal a perfectly coiffed young guy in spotless jeans and a satin bomber jacket.

"Hi! You must be Jaine Austen. I'm Justin, Bebe's personal assistant."

Gaak! What a cutie. True, he was young enough to be my much younger and undoubtedly gay brother, but I couldn't help noticing his full lips, luminous brown eyes, and a most captivating dimple on his left cheek.

"Bebe's waiting for you out back in her studio," he said, flashing me his dimple.

As I followed him inside past a huge living/dining/great room area, I saw the words TEAM BEBE embroidered on the back of his bomber jacket.

At last, we reached a Cordon Bleu–quality kitchen and headed outside into another floral wonderland.

"Hey, Felipe." Justin waved to a gardener bent over a rosebush.

The gardener waved back with a grin, and Justin continued to lead me along a flagstone path to a studio at the back of the property.

We entered through a pair of open French doors into what I can only describe as an oversized walk-in closet—the walls lined with shelves, the shelves lined with designer purses, shoes, and accessories—and racks of dresses scattered everywhere.

Seated in the middle of it all at a sleek white desk was Bebe Braddock, a size-zero blonde, weighed down by a boatload of hair extensions.

Her face was flushed with anger as she shrieked into the phone.

"I'm tired of your excuses. Either pay me what you owe me or I'm going to sic a collection agency on you so fast your head will spin! Understood? . . . Okay. Bye, Mom."

Wait, what? She was talking to her *mother*? What a dreadful woman!

She slammed down the phone, then lit up with pleasure at the sight of me.

"You're Lance's friend, Judy?"

"Actually, it's Jaine."

"Whatever. You're perfect! Absolutely perfect!"

With that, she jumped up from her desk and gave me

a hug, enveloping me in a cloud of industrial strength, migraine-inducing designer perfume—a cross between freesia and lemon-scented Pine-Sol.

"So lovely to meet you!" she gushed, gracing me with a big smile.

Maybe I'd misjudged her. Maybe she wasn't so dreadful.

"Lance told me you were a fashion disaster, but I never dreamed you'd be this bad."

Wait. What?

"I've seen actual train wrecks that look better than you!" she cackled.

Nope, she was dreadful, all right.

"And that hideous T-shirt! What does it say?"

"Cuckoo for Cocoa Puffs," I replied with as much dignity as I could muster.

Lance told me to dress casually. I'd debated between my I ♥ MY CAT T-shirt and CUCKOO FOR COCOA PUFFS. But Cocoa Puffs won out in the end.

"This T-shirt happens to be a collector's item."

"Only if you're a trash collector. Quick, Justin," she said, snapping her fingers. "Take some 'Before' pictures!"

Justin whipped out his cell phone to snap some pictures. I fumed as he snapped away.

"Great!" Bebe cried. "Make that ugly weasel face. It's perfect!"

Justin was finally through snapping pictures when Bebe declared, "If I have to look at that T-shirt one more minute, I may go blind."

And before I knew it, she'd whipped off my precious tee, leaving me standing there in front of Justin in my bra. Which, I noticed with a gulp, had a rather large chocolate stain on one of the cups.

(I really had to stop eating ice cream in my underwear.)

How mortifying, I thought, sneaking a peek at Justin. Thank heavens he was gay.

"Burn it," Bebe said, tossing him my T-shirt.

"Hey, you can't do that!" I protested, as he scooted out of the studio.

"Some day you'll thank me," Bebe said, with a most patronizing smile.

"Here." She reached into a cardboard box on the floor and pulled out a TEAM BEBE bomber jacket. "Put this on."

Then she pressed an intercom button on her desk and barked: "Heidi! Get in here! *Stat!*"

I was on the verge of telling Bebe exactly where she could shove her makeover when she yanked something from one of the clothing racks and held it out to me.

"This might work," she mused.

It was a pale blue cashmere tunic, with tiny seed pearls at the neckline. I reached out to touch it. Never had I felt anything so soft.

"Naturally, I'll have to special-order it in your size. I don't have anything larger than a four here in the studio."

"Yes, please! Order it!" I said, overcome with cashmere lust.

I was standing there, thinking how cute my new sweater would look with skinny jeans when a plump, rosy-cheeked gal, clad in bib overalls and a TEAM BEBE bomber jacket, came rushing into the room.

"There you are, Heidi!" Bebe said. "It's about time. Fashion emergency! Can you possibly do anything with this ghastly mop?"

She poked at my curls with a bony finger.

"Absolutely," Heidi said, shooting me a sympathetic smile. "She's got great hair. Nice and thick." Her own glossy brown hair was cut in a perfect, shoulder-length bob. "What about makeup?"

"Try to highlight her cheekbones if you can find them. And get rid of that ugly brown mole on her chin."

"That's not a mole," Heidi said, peering at my chin. "I think it's chocolate."

Bebe rolled her eyes in disgust. Before she could shoot me another zinger, a heavyset delivery guy came lumbering into the studio with a bunch of dresses in plastic wrap.

"Here's your dry cleaning," he announced.

"Well, don't just stand there. Put it away."

The delivery guy started hanging the dresses on one of the racks when Bebe shouted:

"How many times have I told you? No wire hangers!"

Holy moly. Joan Crawford was alive and well in Brentwood.

"Okay, honey," he said, "just give me a minute, and I'll switch 'em to wooden hangers."

Honey? The dry cleaning guy called Bebe *honey?*

I waited for Bebe to lash out at him, but instead all she said was, "Miles, this is Jaine, that reclamation project I was telling you about. And Jaine, this is my husband, Miles."

Huh? This mountain man was Bebe's husband? Somehow I'd just assumed she'd be married to a Calvin Klein underwear model.

"Nice to meet you," Miles said, reaching out to shake my hand.

"Watch out for chocolate!" Bebe warned. "She's covered in it. The woman's a total mess."

"Don't mind Bebe," Miles said to me. "Good manners aren't her strong suit."

Bebe whirled on him, fire in her eyes.

"Well, excuse me. Sorry if my manners aren't up to snuff. I didn't get a chance to work on them while my house was being bombed in Bosnia. Or when my family came to America with nothing but the clothes on our backs, our valuables sewn into the lining of my mom's coat. Or when I worked my tail off building my business into what it is today."

"Don't blow a gasket, Bebe," Miles said with a sigh.

But Mount Bebe was still erupting.

"Good manners don't pay the bills. I do. And don't you forget it, mister!"

"No worries about that," he said bitterly. "You never let me forget who wears the pants around here."

Yikes. This was a marriage in serious need of counseling.

"When you're through hanging up those dresses," Bebe snapped, "get started on dinner. And don't overcook the pork chops like you did last time."

"Your wish is my command," Miles said, his voice dripping sarcasm.

"Remember," Bebe barreled on, oblivious to his snark. "Not too much olive oil in the salad dressing, absolutely no garlic, no onions, no salt—Omigod, Lacey! How wonderful to see you!"

Dinner prep suddenly forgotten, Bebe was beaming at a gorgeous young thing standing in the doorway.

I recognized the gorgeous young thing right away. It was Lacey Hunt, an up-and-coming movie star whose latest release had garnered rave reviews and an adoring audience. With her red hair, green eyes, and splash of freckles across her pert little nose, Lacey had the kind of innocent girl next door look so appealing to the much sought after 18 to 24 horny young guy demographic.

"Lacey, darling!" Bebe cooed. "Come in."

"Hope I'm not too early for my fitting," Lacey said with a shy smile.

"No, of course not. The others were just leaving."

Then she turned to us, shouting, "Everybody out! Now!"

I was only too happy to oblige, scooting out the door with Heidi and Miles.

As far as I was concerned, my makeover was history.

No way was I about to join the wretched ranks of Team Bebe.

Chapter 2

,

A s Miles shuffled off to the kitchen to get started on his de-flavorized pork chops, Heidi took my arm in hers.

"Let's go to my office and pick out a hair style."

"I don't think so," I demurred. "I can't go through with this makeover. To be perfectly honest, I hate Bebe."

"Don't let that stop you. Everybody does. And besides, I was so looking forward to working with your hair. I love your curls!"

I was flattered that she liked my curls, given that I'd spent half my life trying to tame them into submission.

"C'mon," Heidi urged. "It'll be fun."

What the heck? I figured it couldn't hurt to look at a few hair styles.

Heidi led me to her tiny cell of an office, furnished with only a desk and folding metal chairs. Above the desk was a framed poster of Bebe in designer togs, her hair extensions fanning out behind her, no doubt powered by an unseen wind machine.

"That thing is bolted to the wall," Heidi said, following my gaze. "Impossible to take down. And believe me, I've tried.

"Have a seat," she said, gesturing to one of the metal chairs as she eased her tush onto the other.

"Is Bebe always this bad?" I asked.

"Actually, today's one of her good days."

"You're kidding! How do you stand it?"

"Daily affirmations and fistfuls of Valium."

"Have you ever thought of looking for another job?"

"All the time. In fact, just last week I was offered a terrific studio job, working on an A-list movie. It's a dream come true. I begged Bebe to let me out of my contract, but she won't let me go."

"You're under contract to her?"

"Ironclad," Heidi sighed. "Two years ago, when Bebe offered me the job, I was struggling to pay my rent. So when she dangled a five-year contract in front of me, I jumped to sign it. The pay wasn't great, but I was thrilled to have job security. Little did I know that Bebe wanted to lock me into a contract because no other hair and makeup artist in town would work with her.

"So here I am, stuck with Queen Bebe. In lieu of decent pay, she gives all her employees these stupid bomber jackets and expects us to be over the moon with joy."

With that, she shrugged out of her jacket and tossed it on the back of her chair.

"And every time I hear her yap about how she came to this country as a kid with nothing but the clothes on her back, I want to upchuck. Lord only knows how many people she trampled on her way to the top.

"But enough about Bebe," she said with a grin. "Let's look at some hair styles."

Heidi downloaded a picture of me from my cell phone onto a special software program on her laptop that let us magically see how I was going to look in any given hair style. We spent a highly enjoyable fifteen minutes or so checking out hair styles until we found one we both loved— a shoulder-length bob with beachy waves.

I floated out of Heidi's office on Cloud Nine, imagining myself in my new blue cashmere sweater and beachy hairdo, when I suddenly remembered something that sent me plummeting back down to earth:

My Cuckoo for Cocoa Puffs T-shirt!

What if Justin had followed Bebe's orders and burned it? What if my treasured tee was nothing but a heap of ashes?

I had to find him—and fast!

Fortunately, Justin's office was right next to Heidi's, another sparsely furnished cell with a poster of Bebe above his desk. He was working on his laptop when I came charging into the room.

Thank heavens I didn't smell burnt polyester.

"Where's my T-shirt?" I blurted out.

He looked up at me with his luminous brown eyes, and for a minute, I got sidetracked by how cute he was.

But then I forced myself back to the topic at hand.

"You didn't burn it, did you?"

"Nope, I didn't burn it."

That was the good news.

Then the bad news came skipping out from where it had been waiting in the wings.

"I gave it to Felipe, the gardener."

"You did *what*?"

"Bebe would've killed me if she found out I'd returned it to you. So I gave it to Felipe. He said something about using it as a rag to clean his lawnmower."

"A rag? To clean his lawnmower?" I blanched in horror.

"I'm so sorry. I didn't realize how much the shirt meant to you. He's already left for the day, but I'll call him right now."

He made a quick call to Felipe, who, in a blessed stroke

of good luck, had not yet doused my T-shirt in WD-40. Even better, Felipe promised to hold it for me until I stopped by to get it.

I was weak with relief as Justin gave me Felipe's address.

My beloved T-shirt had been saved!

"I feel so bad about this," Justin said, awash in guilt.

"That's okay."

"No, it's not okay. Let me make it up to you by taking you out."

This accompanied by a most appealing flash of his dimple.

"Out? Like on a date?"

"Yes. On a date."

Yikes. This cutie patootie, at least ten years younger than me, was asking me out. I must admit I was a tad stunned. I'd just assumed that, with his taut trim bod, job in the fashion industry, and dimple that broke the needle on the adorable-o-meter, Justin was of the gay persuasion.

Apparently I'd assumed wrong.

"So how about it?" Justin asked.

Absolutely not. No way. He was far too young for me. I had to ignore the sparkies igniting my day-of-the-week undies and just say no.

"Sounds great," were the words that actually tumbled out of my mouth.

Clearly I've got tapioca where my spine should be.

But who cared if I was a spineless wonder? I had a date with a world-class hottie!

I bid adieu to Justin and headed out to my Corolla, thinking that, between my date with Justin and my beachy new hairdo, maybe this makeover thing would be worth it, after all.

And back I climbed onto Cloud Nine.

Chapter 3

Back home, I found Prozac at her perch on the windowsill, hissing at full throttle.

"Prozac, stop making such a racket over a silly squirrel!"

She turned from the window to glare at me.

I refuse to be silenced—not when the evil alien from the Planet Acorn is plotting world domination!

"For crying out loud, Pro, he's just eating a bagel."

Indeed the squirrel had somehow nabbed a poppy-seed bagel and was nibbling at it with gusto.

Another glare from Prozac.

Today a bagel, tomorrow the world!

Actually, that bagel looked darn tasty. I was tempted to grab one of my own cinnamon raisin bagels to snack on, but then I reminded myself I needed to stay fit and trim for my date with Justin.

No, there would be no bagels in my future.

And I stuck to my word. You'll be proud to know I did not grab a bagel.

Instead I grabbed a pint of Chunky Monkey.

What can I say? I'm nothing if not an unreliable narrator.

I was sitting on the sofa, spooning Chunky Monkey

straight from the carton, thinking about Justin's amazing dimple, when Lance showed up.

"So how'd it go with Bebe?" he asked, zipping past my living room to my kitchen. Seconds later, he returned with a spoon and joined me on the sofa, digging into my Chunky Monkey without a single "may I?"

Oh, well. Better on his hips, where they would soon be burned off at the gym, than on mine, where they would undoubtedly live happily ever after.

"What's up with Prozac?" he asked, as my fractious furball continued her nonstop hissing.

"She's obsessed with a squirrel that's been hanging around the duplex lately, convinced he's evil incarnate."

"Can't you get her to be quiet?"

"I tried, but it's impossible. Trust me. Nothing will shut her up."

Lance turned and shot Prozac a stern look.

"Prozac, be quiet. You're getting on Uncle Lance's nerves."

And just like that, she stopped hissing and came trotting over to the sofa, where she bounded on Lance's lap, batting her big green eyes.

Belly rub, please.

How very annoying. That cat listens to anyone but me.

"So?" Lance asked. "How was Bebe?"

"Awful. Just awful. Rude, arrogant, and downright insulting."

"Funny," Lance simpered, "she's always been wonderful to me. I remember the first time she came to Neiman's and her regular salesman, Sven, was away on vacation. I helped her out, and she was so gaga over me, she dumped Sven in a flash. I don't think he's ever forgiven either one of us.

"People always seem to like me. Cats, too," he added as Prozac purred in his lap. "I'm charismatic. Everyone says so. And you, dear sweet cantankerous Jaine, I'm afraid you're just not a people person."

I refrained from asking why, if he was such a charismatic people person, he was still single.

"What did you think of Justin, Bebe's personal assistant?" Lance asked. "A dreamboat, huh? I've been thinking of asking him out."

"Forget it, Lance. Wrong team."

"What do you mean?"

"He's not gay."

"Don't be silly. Nobody that cute could possibly be straight."

"That's what I thought at first, but he asked me out."

"You?" he gasped, blinking in disbelief. "That's impossible."

You would've thought I'd just told him Ryan Gosling was dating the bearded lady at the circus.

"For your information, Lance, cute guys have been known to ask me out."

"But he's way too young for you."

"How come he's the right age for you but too young for me?"

"Because you're a woman. Everyone knows a thirtysomething woman is fiftysomething in man years."

What utter bilge. I was sorely tempted to bonk him over the head with my spoon, but I needed it to shove ice cream in my mouth.

"Be careful, hon," Lance blathered on. "Lots of young guys dating older women are looking for a sugar mama. Someone to take them to fancy dinners and buy them expensive gifts."

"That's crazy. Justin's way too nice to be a gold digger."

"Dear, sweet, cantankerous, innocent Jaine. All gold diggers seem nice. It's part of their charm. Whatever you do, don't give him money.

"Oops. Gotta run or I'll be late for yoga." he said, nabbing a final scoop of Chunky Monkey before dashing out the door.

I gritted my teeth in annoyance. The nerve of that guy, thinking Justin was a gold digger.

The whole notion was absurd.

But then, as I scraped the bottom of the Chunky Monkey carton for stray banana chunks, doubts began to creep into my mind.

Justin was awfully young—and awfully cute. Why was he interested in a thirtysomething woman in elastic-waist pants and a chocolate-stained bra?

What if Lance was right and Justin was after me for the money I didn't have? What if he was only looking for a sugar mama?

And just like that, I came tumbling down off Cloud Nine.

I swear, that place is harder to stay on than a diet.

You've Got Mail

To: Jausten
From: Shoptillyoudrop
Subject: Exciting news!

Exciting news, darling! The opera is coming to Tampa Vistas! Lydia Pinkus, our ever-resourceful homeowners association president, has arranged for the famed Tampa Bay Opera Company to perform a series of operas right here in the Tampa Vistas clubhouse!

Needless to say, Daddy refuses to go. He claims all that singing gives him a headache. But the real reason he doesn't want to go is Lydia. Anything Lydia organizes, he boycotts. I don't understand what he's got against the poor woman, who devotes so much time and energy to broadening our cultural horizons.

And speaking of culture, we're reading Tolstoy's masterpiece, *War and Peace*, for our women's book club. At least I'm guessing it's a masterpiece. Confidentially, I'm finding it quite a challenge. All those Russian names sound alike to me and I can't seem to get through three pages without falling asleep.

I only hope I'll be able to finish it in time for the meeting. Which, by the way, I'm hosting. I can't decide what to serve for dessert. So far, it's a toss-up between apple crumble and whipped cream fruit parfait.

Must run, sweetheart. Daddy just came home, and he's making a ruckus about something.

XOXO,
Mom

To: Jausten
From: DaddyO
Subject: Fasten Your Seat Belt!

Fasten your seat belt, Lambchop! You're not going to believe what just happened. I was driving home from the supermarket—the same supermarket, by the way, where I once saw Meryl Streep thumping cantaloupes—when I tuned into *Doctor Denise*, one of those radio shrink call-in shows. I wasn't paying much attention until I heard a woman come on the line telling Dr. Denise she was having an affair with a married man.

I was so shocked, I almost swerved into a lamppost. Because the adulterous woman was none other than Lydia Pinkus! I'd recognize The Battle-Axe's grating voice anywhere.

Oh, glorious day! So Ms. High and Mighty Know It All has feet of clay.

As president of the homeowners association, she's an absolute tyrant—Stalin in support hose! This is the woman who banned my "Who Farted?" T-shirt from the clubhouse, who fined Nick Roulakis for painting his house the wrong shade of beige, who shows artsy-fartsy foreign movies with subtitles on Movie Night, and is constantly thinking of ways to torture us with her mind-numbing cultural activities.

Sooner or later (with a little help from me) her affair is bound to become common knowledge.

I can't wait to see her fall from grace!

Love 'n hugs from your ecstatic,
Daddy

PS. Speaking of mind-numbing cultural activities, your mom expects me to go to some stupid opera series Lydia has organized. No way! I hate operas. They never make sense. Any time someone gets stabbed, instead of bleeding, they sing!

**To: Jausten
From: Shoptillyoudrop
Subject: Round the Bend**

Oh, for heaven's sakes. Your daddy has gone totally round the bend. He swears he just heard Lydia Pinkus on the radio, confessing to Dr. Denise that she's having an affair with a married man. Can you believe it? Lydia Pinkus, the moral backbone of Tampa Vistas, having an adulterous affair? I've never heard of anything so preposterous!

If you ask me, Daddy's the one who could use a little help from Dr. Denise.

XOXO
Mom

Chapter 4

The next morning dawned bright and cheery. Very cheery indeed.

In a miraculous turn of events, Prozac seemed to have lost all interest in the evil alien from Planet Acorn.

After a hearty breakfast of minced mackerel guts, she did not resume her perch on the windowsill. Instead she hopped on the sofa to give herself a thorough gynecological exam—totally ignoring the squirrel who was busy burying an orange under my neighbor's azalea bush.

I scarfed down a cinnamon raisin bagel and coffee, reveling in the peace and quiet.

So blissed out was I by the silence that I barely blinked when I read the latest news from my parents. For those of you who haven't already met him, my dad is a FEMA-worthy disaster magnet, the eye of his own personal hurricane. Wherever he goes, chaos seems to follow. Now he was convinced that Lydia Pinkus, a woman known for her impeccable morals and orthopedic sandals, was having an affair with a married man. Daddy's always had it in for Lydia, who, I must admit, can be a bit of a battle-axe. But The Other Woman? Never! Poor Mom. At least she had her book club to distract her.

Shoving all thoughts of my parents aside, I hopped in

the shower and was soon at my computer, working on a flyer for one of my clients, Tip Top Dry Cleaners. (*We clean for you. We press for you. We even dye for you!*) I was singing the praises of their one-hour dry cleaning, urging customers to "stop by and drop your pants," when my mail showed up.

Built some time in the 1940s, my apartment has a vintage mail slot for letters only. Catalogs and packages are left at my front door. I checked the mail and groaned to see several unwanted bills. But I perked up immeasurably after I'd opened my front door and saw my "Fudge of the Month" catalog on my doorstep.

I don't know about you, but I can't think of anything more fun than looking at pictures of fudge. (Except, of course, eating some.)

I was flipping through the glossy pages, stopping to gaze at a mouthwatering walnut brownie creation when a whirling dervish of fur came flying past me.

It was Prozac. The sneaky devil had just pretended to lose interest in the squirrel, when all along she'd been waiting for me to let down my guard and open the front door.

Bloodlust in her eyes, she lunged at the squirrel, who quickly abandoned burying his orange to sprint down the front path.

I was hot on Prozac's heels as she chased the squirrel onto the neighbor's front lawn, where the nimble critter began clambering up a magnolia tree. Prozac was about to clamber up after it, but then we were all distracted—me, the squirrel, and Prozac—by the sound of a woman wailing.

"Omigod! Trevor! Stop!"

I turned to see a towheaded toddler across the street, clutching something in his chubby fist and speed-waddling down a driveway—straight into the path of an oncoming car.

Even more frightening, the car showed no signs of slowing down.

The toddler's mom, her eyes wide with terror, raced after her son.

But before she could get to him, Prozac—channeling her inner Wonder Woman—dashed across the street and jumped up on the toddler, knocking him out of harm's way.

I ran across the street, my heart beating like a bongo, shuddering at the thought of Prozac and the toddler dashing in front of that car. They both could have been killed!

"Omigosh!" said the toddler's mom. "Your cat saved my son's life!"

I beamed with pride. That is, until I looked down and saw what the toddler had been clutching in his hand: a crispy Chicken McNugget—a tasty morsel that Prozac was now gobbling up at the speed of light.

Prozac didn't shove the kid aside to save his life. My greedy furball was only after the McNugget!

"I let go of Trevor's hand to tie my shoelace," the distraught mom was saying, "and the next thing I knew, he was heading straight for that car. And then your heroic cat came to his rescue."

"It's nothing," I assured her, bending over to scoop Prozac in my arms. "Really."

By now, the driver of the car, a gangly teenager, had slammed on his brakes and came running over to join us, along with several neighbors who'd gathered around to see what the commotion was all about.

"I'm so sorry," the teenager said. "I didn't see your little boy."

"That's all right," Trevor's mom said. "This wonderful cat pushed him out of danger."

And everyone began cooing their praises.

"What a brave kitty!"

"So adorable!"

"Look at those big green eyes."

In my arms, Prozac preened.

I'm cuter than Trevor, right?

"I still can't believe it," Trevor's mom was saying. "Your cat saved my son's life. How can I ever thank you?"

Prozac looked up at her, chicken shards still in her whiskers.

Another McNugget would be nice.

Honestly, that cat's nerve knows no bounds.

I assured Trevor's mom that no thanks were necessary and headed back to my apartment, Prozac belching McNugget fumes all the way home.

Chapter 5

"Ugh! You look like a tugboat in that dress."

I was standing on a pedestal in Bebe's studio, trapped in a cloud of her Pine-Sol perfume, bombarded by a barrage of insults.

So far, in what appeared to be a nautically themed onslaught, I'd been compared to a tugboat, a barge, and a battleship. Also, Elsie the Cow and Bigfoot.

Even worse than her insults was the torturous spandex body shaper she made me squeeze myself into. For the purposes of this narrative and to avoid a pesky lawsuit, let's call them Spunx.

The "tugboat" dress Bebe hated was one I personally liked. A cute A-line number that, had I not been bound by those godawful Spunx, would have given me plenty of room to breathe.

But Bebe didn't give a hoot about my respiratory system. She'd gone gaga over a fitted ruched dress that she insisted took inches off my hips. (And years off my life, no doubt, if my organs continued to be scrunched together like sumo wrestlers in a Volkswagen.)

Kneeling at my feet throughout the whole ordeal was Bebe's seamstress, Anna, a mouse of a woman with pins in her mouth and a whipped dog look in her eyes.

"Pinch the waistband tighter!" Bebe had barked at her earlier when I'd tried on a pair of itchy wool slacks.

"But I can't breathe," I'd protested.

"Good. You've got to suffer for beauty."

Anna shot me an apologetic look as she tightened the waistband with some straight pins.

Oh, well. At least Bebe had decided to keep the blue cashmere tunic I'd lusted after on my last visit.

"It actually doesn't look horrible on you," Bebe said, her idea of a compliment.

A few more outfits were tried on and insults hurled before Bebe was satisfied with her selections and gave me permission to change back into my own clothes.

I scooted to a curtained-off changing room in the corner of the studio and eagerly wiggled out of those damned Spunx. As I changed back into my beloved elastic-waist jeans, I heard Bebe barking at Anna:

"Get those alterations done ASAP. And no screwups. One more uneven hem and you're history!"

In another life, I bet she goose-stepped with the Gestapo.

When I emerged from the dressing room, Anna had gone, and Bebe was eyeing one of the dress racks, jaw clenched and temples throbbing.

Uh-oh. Looked like Mount Bebe was about to erupt.

"Another wire hanger!" she cried, grabbing the offending piece of metal and waving it in the air.

"Miles!" she screeched into her intercom. "Get in here right away!"

Seconds later, the studio doors opened, but it wasn't Miles.

Instead, an older woman—with badly dyed jet-black hair, way too much makeup, and a designer suit that had seen better days—came storming into the studio on scuffed stilettos.

"You bitch!" she hissed at Bebe, as Miles raced in after her.

"I tried to stop her," Miles said, "but she pushed right past me."

"You couldn't stop her? A former linebacker? How useless can one man be?" She shook her head in disgust. "And by the way, I found another wire hanger on the rack." She hurled it at him, almost nicking him in the forehead. "Get rid of it!"

Then she turned to the older woman.

"What's your problem, Tatiana?"

"I'll tell you what my problem is. You stole Lacey Hunt right out from under me."

"So what if I did?" Bebe shot back, showing zero signs of remorse.

"In case you've forgotten," Tatiana cried, quivering with indignation, "I gave you your start in this business. When you and I first met, you were nothing but a personal shopper at Macy's, buying athleisure suits for soccer grandmas. I gave you a job! I gave you a career—"

Her eyes were now riveted on a crimson leather handbag on one of Bebe's shelves. I figured it was nosebleed expensive, embellished as it was by what looked like genuine gold hardware.

"—I gave you that Birken purse! And this is how you repay me? By stealing my client? Heaven only knows what dirty trick you used to lure Lacey away from me."

"Oh, please," Bebe scoffed. "Lacey couldn't wait to make the switch and dump you. Newsflash, Tatiana: Your career's over. Finished. Kaput. Has been for ages. Rumor has it the last celebrity you dressed was Betsy Ross."

This was one insult too many for Tatiana.

"You miserable ingrate!" she cried, charging at Bebe, her face a frightening beet red.

Lucky for Bebe, Miles managed to intercept her and pull her away.

"Get her out of here right now," Bebe said, "before I call the police."

"C'mon, Tatiana." Miles took the older woman by the elbow. "It's best you go."

As Miles led her out of the studio, Tatiana turned to Bebe and hurled her parting shot.

"I'll get you for this, Bebe. I swear I will."

"Yeah, right," Bebe shot back. "I'm shaking in my shoes."

But I couldn't help noticing a look of fear in her eyes.

Tatiana sure seemed out for revenge, and I, for one, wouldn't have wanted to be on the receiving end of her rage.

"Okay, show's over," Bebe said, turning to me when Tatiana had gone. "I'll call you when the alterations are ready. And leave the Spunx here. I don't want you stretching them out."

Tossing the Spunx on Bebe's desk, I scurried out of the studio, thrilled to be rid of Bebe and her spandex torture chamber. I was just about to head down the side of the house to the front gate when Miles called out to me from the kitchen.

"Hey, Jaine. Don't leave yet. Heidi wants to see you."

He beckoned me into the kitchen, where I was surprised to see Tatiana sitting at a ginormous kitchen island, sipping from a steaming mug of tea.

All traces of the rage she'd spewed in the studio had vanished, replaced by an air of defeat. Drawn and haggard, she sat hunched over her mug, makeup caked in her wrinkles, her jet-black hair wilting under its helmet of hair spray.

"Come join us, Jaine," Miles said. "Have a brownie."

He pointed to a plate of ooey-gooey goodies in the center of the island.

"They're fresh from the oven."

As I could tell, by the mouthwatering aroma of chocolate wafting through the air. But I couldn't possibly have one. Not if I expected to squeeze myself into my skintight makeover outfits.

"No, thanks. I'm fine."

"Have some tea then," he said, pouring some into a mug from a teapot on the stove.

I took the tea and hoisted myself up onto a stool next to Tatiana.

An unfinished brownie sat in front of her, studded with nuts and slathered with a thick layer of frosting.

It was all I could do not to snatch it up and scarf it down.

"Hit me again, honey," she said to Miles, holding out her cup.

Miles did not reach for the teapot but for a bottle of bourbon and poured some into her mug.

"Want some, Jaine?" Miles asked, holding out the bottle.

After what I'd just been through, I could've used a jolt of Jim Beam, but I opted for sobriety.

Miles joined us at the island and helped himself to a brownie.

"I don't get it," Tatiana was saying. "After all I've done for Bebe, how can she be so cruel?"

"Years of practice," Miles replied with a grim smile.

"How do you live with her?"

"It isn't easy. I try to remember the good times in high school—back when I was a football player and Bebe was the cutest girl on the cheerleading squad.

"She was different then," he said, a faraway look in his eyes. "So much nicer."

"Or maybe she was always a bitch," Tatiana said, "but you were too blinded by hormones to see it."

"Maybe," Miles sighed.

"I'd better get moving before Bebe catches me here and goes ballistic." Tatiana got down from the stool, smoothing the jacket of her tattered suit. "Thanks for the tea, Miles. You make it just the way I like it."

"Wait!" He jumped up and reached into his pocket for his wallet, then handed her a generous wad of cash.

She hesitated a beat. But only a beat.

"I shouldn't," she said, taking the cash, "but I won't lie. I need the money."

Then she threw her arms around Miles and gave him a hug.

"You're too good for her, Miles. Way too good."

I had to agree with her on that one.

With a feeble wave good-bye, she turned and headed down the hallway.

"I should be going, too," I said, getting up from my stool.

Okay, so I didn't get up from my stool. I stayed to finish my brownie. (Okay, two brownies.)

You didn't really think I was going to resist the lure of ooey-gooey chocolate, did you?

Chapter 6

The door to Heidi's office was shut when I got there, an odd thunking noise coming from inside.

"Heidi," I called out. "It's me, Jaine."

"Come on in!"

I opened the door to find Heidi hurling a suction-cup dart at the framed poster of Bebe hanging over her desk. So that explained the thunking noise.

"Bingo!" Heidi cried as her dart made contact with the poster. "Straight to her heart. She's a goner for sure."

Then she hurled another.

"Boom! Right on her nose job! Wanna try?" she asked, holding out a dart.

"No, I'm good."

"Well, I'm not. I got another call from the studio this morning, offering me even more money to leave Bebe and go work for them. I begged Bebe to let me out of my contract, but she still refuses to let me go."

"I'm so sorry," I said.

"Not as sorry as I am."

She lobbed another missile at the poster, this one landing on Bebe's chest.

"Yippee! There go her implants!"

"You wanted to see me?" I reminded her as she went to retrieve the darts.

"Right. Let me show you some tweaks I made to your hair style."

She opened her laptop and showed me the tweaks—more beachy waves and longer bangs—all of which I loved.

"It looks fabulous!"

"And one more thing. Before I cut your hair, I'd like you to start giving yourself deep-conditioning olive oil treatments. Just massage some olive oil in your hair, cover it with a shower cap for about twenty minutes, then shampoo. It'll make your hair amazingly soft and shiny."

"Sounds good."

If it made my hair even half as shiny as Heidi's sleek bob, I'd be in heaven.

"Well," I said, wrenching my eyes from the image of the new, improved me on Heidi's laptop, "time for me to get going."

"Are you sure you don't want to give the darts a try?"

She held them out to me, a mischievous glint in her eyes.

"Okay, maybe I will."

I took one of the darts and threw it, feeling a groundswell of joy when it made contact with the poster.

"Yes!" Heidi high-fived me. "Right in her crotch! That has to hurt! Isn't this the best game ever?"

"You betcha!" I said, reaching for another dart and hurling it with gusto.

After a few more gratifying rounds of mutilating Bebe, I bid Heidi a fond farewell.

On my way to the front door, I peeked in Justin's office and swallowed a pang of disappointment to find he wasn't there. But I perked up immeasurably when I walked outside and saw him heading up the path with some garment bags.

"Hey, you!" he said, flashing me his dimple.

Aack. My knees went a tad wobbly.

"I thought maybe we could hang out tomorrow night."

Yesyesyesyesyes! were the words I managed not to screech.

"How about it?" he said.

"I'm not sure," I lied shamelessly, trying to seem like someone whose social sked was packed with fun events. "Let me check my calendar." I opened my cell phone where the only listing for the next night was pizza and *Downton Abbey*.

"Why, yes, I think I can make it."

"Great!" he beamed, treating me to another glimpse of his dimple. "Text me your address, and I'll pick you up at ten."

"Ten?" I gulped. "At night?"

"Sure, that's when all the clubs get hopping."

Holy moly. Welcome to the world of Gen Z dating.

I only hoped I'd stay awake long enough for a good-night kiss.

Chapter 7

I'm happy to report that the gang at Tip Top Dry Cleaners liked my "Drop Your Pants" flyer so much, they hired me to write a bunch of radio spots.

Yay, me!

I spent the next morning at my desk (otherwise known as my dining room table) banging away on the commercials, the air filled with the sweet sounds of Prozac snoring on the sofa.

There'd been no sign of the Evil Alien from Planet Acorn, and Prozac was quite pleased with herself, no doubt convinced she'd scared off the critter for good.

I must confess my mind was wandering just a tad as I wrote the Tip Top spots. I kept thinking about Justin and our date that night. I still couldn't believe he was picking me up at ten. That's usually when I'm curled up in bed with an episode of *House Hunters*. I'd have to take a nap if I expected to stay awake until the wee hours.

Leaving Tip Top temporarily in limbo, I drew up the following schedule:

Work until 6:00 PM (with time out for lunch)
6:00–8:00 PM: Rejuvenating nap
8:00–8:30: Dinner

8:30–10:00 PM: Soak in tub, wash hair, exfoliate, moisturize, get dressed in fabulous club-hopping outfit, blow out hair, apply makeup, spritz perfume, and magically morph from dry cleaning drudge to club scene queen.

My schedule set, I resumed work on Tip Top.

At around one o'clock, I broke for lunch, treating myself to a nutritious southwest grilled chicken salad from McDonald's, with just the weensiest side of fries. Okay, it wasn't so weensy, but I felt quite noble having eaten so much lettuce in one sitting.

I'd just finished scarfing down the last fry and was licking ketchup from my fingers when Lance came banging at my front door.

"Open up, Jaine! Major news!"

I rose with a groan. Lance's idea of major news is getting right-swiped on Tinder.

The minute I opened the door, he came whooshing in, waving his cell phone and making a beeline for Prozac.

"Prozac, sweetie, you're a star!"

At the sound of her name, Prozac perked up.

"Look!" Lance said, shoving the phone in my face. "Somebody took this video of Prozac—The Cat Who Saved a Toddler's Life!"

There on his phone was a video of Prozac racing across the street and pushing Trevor, the toddler with the Chicken McNugget, out from the path of the oncoming car.

"Prozac!" Lance squealed. "You're a hero. You saved a toddler's life!"

Prozac preened.

Not only that, I vanquished the Evil Alien from Planet Acorn.

"The video's already got more than a thousand views," Lance gushed. "Isn't it wonderful?"

No, it wasn't wonderful. Not in the least. The video made it look like Prozac was actually trying to protect Trevor when she knocked him out of harm's way, totally leaving out the part where she swan dived into his Mc-Nugget. Instead, the buttinsky who shot the video focused on Trevor's grateful mom, hugging her child—and then, most annoyingly, panned to a ghastly close-up of my tush as I bent down to pick up Prozac.

"My furry princess!" Lance cried, scooping Prozac in his arms and taking a selfie with her.

"Oh, please. Prozac didn't try to save the toddler. She pushed him away so she could get at his Chicken Mc-Nugget."

"I refuse to believe that," said Lance, aghast. "Not my angel Prozac!"

Nestled in his arms, Prozac gazed at me with slitted eyes.

Sure have him fooled, don't I?

"Far be it from me to criticize you, Jaine—"

"Then don't."

"—but you're just jealous because Pro got all the attention, and all you got was a close-up of your tush."

He was right, of course. That shot of my tush appeared to take up the entire screen.

Somehow I managed to pry Prozac from Lance's arms and shove him gently out the door.

Then I returned to my computer, determined to devote the rest of the day to Tip Top. But all I could think of was my tush in cyberspace. Thank goodness my face was hardly visible in the shot.

Surely, no one would recognize me.

Au contraire.

I hadn't finished my very first Oreo (okay, I was stress-eating) when the phone started ringing off the hook. I got calls from classmates I hadn't seen since my days at Hermosa High; from former boyfriends ("I'd know that tush anywhere!"); and from Cryo-suction, a delightful company offering to freeze my fat cells for only five thousand dollars.

Oh, Lord! My tush was going viral. I only prayed Justin hadn't seen the video.

After a few more phone calls, I disconnected the phone and finally got some writing done.

By the time six o'clock rolled around, I was feeling a lot calmer—thanks to the distractive powers of work (and Oreos).

I crawled into bed for my nap and was just about to doze off when I was jerked awake by a loud banging at my front door.

Damn that Lance, I thought, certain he'd returned to annoy me with a Prozac news alert.

But it wasn't Lance. It was a delivery guy with a cellophane-wrapped gift basket from Trevor's mom, filled with kitty treats and toys.

Prozac bolted over to it and began sniffing it eagerly.

I took a sniff, too, and recognized the minty smell of catnip coming from a toy mouse.

Her eyes wide with catnip fever, Prozac looked up at me and meowed.

Open this gift basket! Ipso pronto!

But I couldn't possibly open it and have Prozac ricocheting around my apartment, high on catnip. Not if I wanted to get any sleep.

"Not now, Pro. I'll open it later."

She practically gasped in disbelief.

You're saying no to The Cat Who Saved a Toddler's Life?

Ignoring her filthy look, I stowed the basket on the top shelf of my coat closet, firmly closing the door, and headed back to my bedroom.

Once again, I was drifting off to sleep when I heard a loud crash.

I ran out to the living room to find the closet door open, the gift basket on the floor, Prozac clawing at the cellophane.

Why was I not surprised?

My ingenious kitty had long ago mastered the art of leaping onto doorknobs and opening doors.

Now she ripped open the cellophane and retrieved the catnip-filled mouse, batting it around with all the gusto of a World Series champ.

There was no way I was going to be able to keep this toy from Prozac.

Resigned, I trudged back to bed.

Needless to say, I did not drop off into the restful slumber I'd been hoping for.

Instead I lay there, visions of my tush dancing in my head, accompanied by the piercing squeaks of the toy mouse as Prozac pummeled it to oblivion.

Eventually I managed to doze off and got approximately ten measly minutes of sleep before my alarm went off.

Not the least bit rejuvenated, I hauled myself out of bed and headed for the kitchen to fix myself dinner: a frozen mini-pepperoni and garlic pizza, only 390 calories a serving. I started reading the ingredients label on the box—tomatoes, pepperoni, extra virgin olive oil—and remembered

Heidi's suggestion about giving myself an olive oil hair treatment.

What a great idea. I'd put some on my hair and let it soak in while I was eating dinner. And voilà! I'd have silky-soft tresses for my date with Justin.

After putting the pizza in the oven, I began rummaging in my cupboard for olive oil.

I vaguely recalled buying some when, in one of my rare fits of domesticity, I attempted to make a rosemary lemon chicken. An attempt that went spectacularly awry when I forgot to remove the plastic packet of giblets from inside the chicken.

But I could swear I'd used olive oil in that recipe. And indeed I found a bottle shoved in the back of my cupboard.

I retrieved it eagerly and began massaging it into my hair.

By now, my pizza was heating up, smelling of pepperoni and garlic. A whole lot of garlic. My kitchen was reeking of the stuff.

And suddenly I realized that the garlic I smelled was not coming from my pizza, but from my hair.

I grabbed the bottle of olive oil and took a close look at the label. For the first time I noticed, in small print, the pivotal words "Garlic Infused."

Holy mackerel. I smelled like the exhaust vent at a pizzeria.

This would never do for my date with Justin.

So I dashed into the shower and began washing my hair. But the olive oil was greasy stuff. It took three rounds of sudsing to get rid of it.

At least, I thought I got rid of it.

After blowing my hair dry, I could still smell it.

It took me two more trips to the shower to finally wash it away.

Which meant, of course, that I did not have time to luxuriate in the tub, shave my legs, or tweeze my eyebrows. Exfoliation had bitten the dust, along with any shred of relaxation.

Nor did I have time to rummage around in my closet and put together a fabulous club-hopping outfit. Instead I threw on a pair of elastic-waist skinny jeans and the first tunic I saw—a flowy black jersey number.

All that mattered was that it covered my tush. Which, according to my latest check on YouTube, had accrued more than two thousand views. No way was my fanny getting any more exposure that night.

By now, it was almost 9:30.

I frantically spritzed on perfume, slapped on some lipstick, and shoved my feet into my one and only pair of Manolos.

With no time to blow-dry my hair, I scrunched it into what I hoped was a sexy mop of curls gone wild.

I was surveying myself in the mirror when all of a sudden, I smelled something burning.

My pizza! I'd forgotten all about it!

I raced to the kitchen past Prozac, who was conked out on the sofa, exhausted from her battle with the catnip mouse.

Great. *Now* she was sleeping. The Cat Who Saved a Toddler's Life couldn't be bothered to let me know my apartment was about to catch fire.

In the kitchen, I pulled the charred remains of my pizza from the oven.

Just as I was tossing it in the trash, there was a knock on my door.

Oh, crud. Justin. And I hadn't had a thing to eat. (Except for the two Oreos I'd just shoved in my mouth.)

I hurried to the door, gulping down the Oreos, praying I didn't have unsightly globs of chocolate on my teeth.

Having barely survived the charred pizza and olive oil disasters, I must admit I was a tad frazzled when I opened the door.

But the sight of Justin standing there—looking fab in tight jeans and TEAM BEBE bomber jacket, his hair slicked back from a shower—was just the pick-me-up I needed.

"Come in!" I managed to croak.

He stepped inside and sniffed.

"Do I smell something burning?"

"Just a minor culinary disaster. I specialize in those."

"Me too," he grinned, treating me to a dazzling glimpse of his dimple. "I'm still figuring out how to nuke water."

I melted at the sight of that dimple, suddenly weak in the knees.

And I wasn't the only one smitten.

Prozac, the shameless hussy, had hurled herself at his ankles, rubbing against him with wild abandon, a kitty porn star in the making.

Hubba hubba, what a hottie. And so young! Then, shooting me a sidelong glance. *Much too young for you!*

"Aren't you a pretty kitty," Justin said, picking her up.

She purred in ecstasy as he scratched her behind her ears.

You bet I am! Now rub my belly!

"Gee," he said, gazing down at her, "she looks awfully familiar. I feel like I've seen her before."

"No," I insisted. "Not possible. She's got a very common kitty face. I'm sure you've never seen her before."

Pro meowed in protest.

She lies! I'm The Cat Who Saved a Toddler's Life!

"Well, let's get moving," I said, eager to sidetrack any discussion of Prozac's video. "We don't want to be late for the club."

"I hope you like to dance," Justin said.

"Absolutely," I lied, dreading the thought of navigating the dance floor in my four-inch Manolos.

"Okay, Pro," I said, reaching for her. "Justin and I have to go."

A yowl of protest.

Wait. He still hasn't rubbed my belly!

Somehow I managed to pry her away from Justin and deposit her on the sofa, where she gave me the stink eye royale.

Somebody's going to find an unpleasant surprise in her slippers tonight.

Ignoring the threat of a revenge poop, I hurried Justin out the door.

A cute red Fiat was parked out front, a perfect fit with Justin's sexy metrosexual look.

But Justin led me past the Fiat to a flimsy-looking motorcycle.

"Here we are," he said, with a flourish. "My trusty steed. Hope you like riding on motorbikes."

"Absolutely," I lied again, picturing my lifeless body sprawled on a freeway after a deadly encounter with a big rig.

"Put this on," he said, unhooking a helmet from under his motorcycle seat.

Bye-bye, curls gone wild. Now I'd be stuck with helmet hair all night.

I put on the helmet and climbed behind him on the motorbike.

"Hold on tight!" he said, pulling my arms around his hot bod.

At last! Something fun!

I held onto him as instructed, my arms around his torso, a surge of warmies in my day-of-the-week undies.

Then, just as I nestled closer, feeling that this night might turn out to be quite wonderful, Justin sniffed the air and said, "I smell garlic."

Damn that olive oil!

Chapter 8

To this day, I still don't know the exact location of the club Justin took me to, because I spent the entire ride over with my eyes squeezed shut, waiting to be hurtled to my death.

"Isn't this fun?" Justin had called out at one point.

"Yes, fun," I croaked, my heart pounding almost as fast as the cars I heard whizzing by on what sounded like a freeway.

When we finally showed up at the club, I was so thrilled to be alive, I didn't even care that my garlic-scented hair had been ironed flat by my helmet.

Justin led me inside a barn of a building with a bar at one end and high tables and stools circling a huge dance floor. Strobe lights were flashing colorful stripes onto the couples dancing, all of them younger—much younger—than me.

My eardrums and I were grateful when Justin nabbed us a table in a far corner of the room, away from the blaring speakers.

"So what do you think?" Justin asked. "It's crazy, right?"

"Crazy," I echoed with a wan smile, wondering what

the heck I was doing in a room full of kids just a stone's throw from puberty.

"Would you like something from the bar?" he asked.

"A Chardonnay would be great."

"I'll have a Sam Adams," Justin said. Then, with a sheepish grin, he added: "Would you mind buying the drinks? I'm only twenty. They won't sell me booze."

Only twenty? I knew he was young, but not that young!

"Okay, sure," I said, getting down off my stool.

And as I headed for the bar, I remembered what Lance said about young guys on the hunt for sugar mamas. Was that what this was all about? Was I just a meal ticket? I should have guessed this whole Justin thing was too good to be true.

At the bar, I gave our order to one of the hipster bartenders. By now, of course, I was starving. It was almost eleven, and I still hadn't eaten any dinner.

"Can I see a menu?" I asked.

"Sorry, ma'am." *Ma'am? Did he just call me "ma'am"?* "We don't serve food here."

No food? He had to be kidding!

So when he turned his back to get the drinks, I reached over and nabbed some maraschino cherries. I barely managed to scarf them down when he returned with the wine and the beer.

"That'll be twenty-three dollars. Twenty for the drinks. And three for the cherries," he added with a smirk.

I grudgingly forked over twenty-five bucks, resenting every cent of the two dollar tip I felt obliged to give him.

When I returned to our table, I found Justin chatting with a cute young thing in skintight leggings and halter top, her hair dyed neon pink.

"Hey," Justin said to me. "This is my friend Mitzi. She models for Bebe sometimes."

"Omigosh!" the neon-haired Barbie cried. "You must be Justin's mom! He's told me so much about you!"

Justin's *mom*? For crying out loud, I couldn't possibly look that old, could I? And then, with a sinking sensation, it occurred to me that, given Justin's age, it was technically possible.

I felt more foolish than ever for agreeing to go out with him.

"Jaine's not my mom, Mitzi. She's my date."

That said with his arm sliding around my waist.

Oh dear. His arm around my waist sure felt nice. But no, I couldn't let myself get sucked into Justinland. No way was I about to become anyone's sugar mama.

"Oops. My mistake," Mitzi said, her blush almost as bright as her hair. "Well, see you round, Justin."

And off she skipped with a fluttery wave.

"Here you go," I said, sliding out from Justin's arm and putting the drinks on the table.

As I climbed onto my stool, Justin reached into his pocket and pulled out his wallet.

"This ought to cover it," he said, slapping two twenties on the table.

Yes! He was paying for the drinks! He wasn't looking for a sugar mama after all. Damn that Lance for planting the seed of doubt in my mind.

"That's way too much," I said, pushing one of the twenties back at him.

"I insist," he said, shoving it back at me. "It's my pleasure. Honest."

I was sitting there, basking in the glow of his smile,

when he said, "Mitzi's a nice kid, but she's so immature. Like most women my age. That's why I prefer dating older women."

That would be moi.

"My last girlfriend was twenty-six. That's about your age, right?"

"Close," I had the audacity to lie. "Twenty-seven."

Clearly I was missing the all-important transparency gene.

"Here's to older women," Justin said, clinking my wine-glass with his beer bottle.

"To older women," I echoed.

"It's funny," he said, sniffing. "I keep smelling garlic. Don't you?"

I couldn't possibly tell one more lie or some angel in a position of authority would come down from heaven and slap me silly.

"Actually," I confessed, "it's coming from my hair."

"Your hair?" He blinked in surprise.

"Heidi suggested that I give my hair an olive oil conditioning treatment, and I doused my head with the stuff before I realized it was 'garlic infused.' "

"Cool!" He leaned across the table to take a whiff of my hair. "I love garlic!"

He loved garlic! Yes! We were culinary soulmates!

"One of my favorite foods is garlic and pepperoni pizza," he said. "The other two are Oreos and kale salad."

Two out of three wasn't bad.

"You in the mood for pizza?" he asked.

"Always."

"Let's get some."

"But they don't serve food here."

"No problem," he said, taking out his cell phone. "I'll

have it delivered." And just like that, he was on Grubhub ordering pizzas and Cokes.

Bless him! Suddenly the club, which had, up to now, seemed impossibly loud and way too hip for the likes of *moi*, seemed warm and welcoming. Maybe I could pull off this younger vibe after all.

Our pizzas soon arrived, and before long we were gabbing away between bites of garlic and pepperoni.

"So what's it like working for Bebe?" I asked, wondering if Justin belonged to the I Hate Bebe club.

"It's not so bad," he said. "I've learned how to tune her out when she's on one of her rampages. And the pay's pretty good, much better than I'd be earning as a barista. Best of all, I get this fabulous TEAM BEBE bomber jacket," he added with a laugh.

"Are you planning on pursuing a career in the fashion industry?"

"Heck, no. I'm studying to be a classical violinist."

Let's take stock here, shall we? He was adorable, loved pizza, and was a violin prodigy to boot. No doubt about it. I'd hit the dating jackpot.

"In fact," he was saying, "I would have asked you to a performance of Beethoven's Violin Concerto No. 9 tonight, but most women aren't interested in that stuff."

"Oh, I simply adore classical music!" I said, back on my lying streak, a woman who wouldn't know Beethoven's Violin Concerto No. 9 if it came and sat on my lap.

"Really? Would you like to come to my violin recital next Thursday?"

"I'd love it!"

"It's a date. Now what do you say we get out on that dance floor?"

By then I was on such a high, I didn't even flinch at the

prospect of navigating the dance floor on my four-inch Manolos.

"I just need to make a quick trip to the ladies' room," I said, the wine and Coke having rushed through my urinary tract at Indy 500 speed.

"Okay. Meet you on the dance floor."

I got up and hustled to the ladies' room, where I checked myself in the mirror and was happy to see my hair was not nearly as flat as I thought it would be. After a quick tinkle, I washed my hands, refreshed my lipstick, and made my way back out to the club.

Everyone seemed to be in a wonderful mood, giggling and laughing as I headed for the dance floor.

Justin was there waiting for me.

"Ready to show 'em how it's done?" he asked.

"You betcha!" I replied, still aware of people giggling nearby. In fact, the giggling had grown a lot louder. What the heck was so funny? I wondered.

I was about to find out.

"Hey!" someone shouted, pointing at my tush. "You're the lady whose cat saved a toddler's life!"

I turned around to check my tush and realized that in my haste to return to Justin, I'd accidentally tucked the back of my tunic into my elastic-waist jeans.

Once again, my fanny was on display for all the world to see.

Mortified, I quickly pulled the tunic out from where it was trapped in my jeans. But not quick enough to stop Justin from taking a peek at my fanny.

"I thought I recognized Prozac earlier," he said. "That was her in the video. And you, too, right?"

"Yes," I nodded, shamefaced.

"Why didn't you tell me?"

"I was embarrassed about that awful shot of me bending over at the end."

"Are you kidding?" Justin said, shooting me a lethal dose of his dimple. "That was my favorite part!"

Omigosh. It was his favorite part! Justin liked my tush!

With happy heart, I sashayed out to the dance floor and proceeded to shake it with gusto.

You've Got Mail

To: Jausten
From: DaddyO
Subject: Hot on the Trail

I've been quite the gumshoe these past few days, Lambchop, hot on the trail of The Battle-Axe—disguised in a baseball cap and nifty aviator sunglasses I bought at the 99 cent store. At first it was pretty boring, following Stinky Pinkus to the library, the historical society, and the stupid health food shop where she stocks up on wheat germ.

But today I finally got lucky, following her to the mall, where she popped into Victoria's Secret. Yes, *that* Victoria's Secret, home of the push-up bra and lace garter belt. Fifteen minutes later, she came sailing out, a Victoria's Secret shopping bag swinging from her arm. If I had even a shred of a doubt before, it was swept away today. The Battle-Axe is having an affair for sure!

Now all I have to do is prove it.

Love 'n hugs
From your intrepid,
Daddy

To: Jausten
From: Shoptillyoudrop
Subject: Too Much Rockford!

Oh, my stars. Your daddy has been watching far too many *Rockford Files* reruns. He's been tailing Lydia for days, wearing the most ridiculous pair of oversized sunglasses he bought at the 99 cent store, hoping to catch her in the arms of her "married lover."

Today he came home, all excited because he saw Lydia coming out of Victoria's Secret with a shopping bag. He's convinced she's buying sexy lingerie for her adulterous trysts. Of all the ridiculous notions! Just because she stopped in at Victoria's Secret doesn't mean she's having an affair. Why, just last year I bought an adorable Victoria's Secret hoodie, the perfect topper for my Home Shopping Club sequined pink capri set.

Besides, Lydia has no time for an affair. She's busy handling some important family matters and has appointed me to lead this month's book club. I'm flattered, of course, but I still haven't made it past chapter one of *War and Peace*. There's no way I can finish that mountain of a book in time for the meeting. I'll just have to read the plot highlights on Wikipedia.

I've decided to have the meeting out on the patio and serve wine spritzers along with my whipped cream fruit parfait, which should look lovely in my beautiful crystal parfait bowl. Maybe with all those calories and wine, the gals won't care that I haven't finished (or barely even started) the book.

XOXO,
Mom

To: Jausten
From: DaddyO
Subject: Just the Beginning

My Victoria's Secret discovery is just the beginning. I'm determined to catch The Battle-Axe in the arms of her married lover. (Although why any man would choose to have a fling with The Battle-Axe, I'll never know. She has all the allure of a Sherman tank.)

Gotta run, Lambchop. *Rockford Files* is on!

Love 'n snuggles from,
Daddy

To: Jausten
From: Shoptillyoudrop

Just started reading the plot summary of *War and Peace* on Wikipedia, and I still can't keep all those Russian names straight! This will never do!

XOXO,
Mom

Chapter 9

Wake up! Wake up!

I opened a bleary eye the next morning to find Prozac pawing at my chest in a frenzy.

Time to fix breakfast for your beloved kitty!

It was six AM, and I'd gotten all of three hours of sleep.

"Go away, Pro. It's time you learned to use a can opener and fix your own breakfast."

An indignant meow.

It's not my fault you stayed out half the night, leaving me alone with nothing to do but rip a new hole in your quilt.

Indeed I looked over and saw a fresh lump of stuffing sprouting from my quilt.

With a weary sigh, I got of bed, carefully checking for an unwanted surprise in my slippers. You'll be happy to know Prozac did not make good on her threat to poop in them.

(Instead, as I was later to learn, she pooped in my running shoes.)

In the kitchen, I sloshed a can of Minced Mackerel Guts into her bowl and put it down in front of her.

She sniffed at it dismissively.

Minced mackerel guts? For The Cat Who Saved a Toddler's Life? Outrageous! Make me eggs Benedict and make it snappy!

"You'll eat minced mackerel guts and like it, young lady."

I guess she could tell I meant business because, after giving me the stink eye, she proceeded to swan dive into her chow.

Leaving her sucking up mackerel guts, I hurried back to bed and drifted off into a delicious sleep. I'm ashamed to admit I did not wake up until one o'clock that afternoon. And even then, I didn't get out bed. Instead I lay there for another half hour, a goofy smile on my face, thinking about my date with Justin.

After a glorious session on the dance floor, I rode home on the back of Justin's motorcycle, my arms wrapped around his waist, feeling the heat of his body against mine.

Back at my duplex, he walked me up the path to my front door.

"Well, good night," he said. "I had fun."

And with that he started back down the path.

That was it? He had fun? After I'd practically grown an umbilical cord to his abs, was he blowing me off?

Then before I knew it, he whirled around and was back at my side, sweeping me up in a wowie-zowie good-night kiss I wouldn't soon forget, lust bubbles bursting all over my body.

"I shouldn't have done that," he said, breaking away, "but you were just so irresistible, I couldn't stop myself."

Omigosh! I was irresistible!

Then he swept me up into another swoon-worthy smacker.

When we finally came up for air, he said, "I'd better go. I've got work tomorrow."

Don't go! I felt like wailing, but I managed to rein in my hormones and let myself into my apartment, still reeling from his kisses.

Now, lying in bed, I wondered if maybe this younger man thing could work out. Hadn't Audrey Hepburn, Susan Sarandon, and Demi Moore all hooked up with younger men? And what about Queen Victoria and her boy toy, John Brown? This kind of romance happened all the time. Why not to me?

I thought of how cute Justin was, his lofty musical ambitions, his great moves on the dance floor, and his even better moves on my front doorstep. I was ready to take the plunge.

In a happy glow, I floated off to the kitchen to nuke myself a cinnamon raisin bagel. (Okay, two cinnamon raisin bagels.) Dee-lish, especially with gobs of butter and strawberry jam.

Once I'd scraped every last crumb from my plate, I parked myself at my computer where, believe it or not, I managed to tear my thoughts away from Justin long enough to open my emails. Which I instantly regretted, cringing at the thought of Daddy tailing Lydia Pinkus to Victoria's Secret.

But I refused to spoil my good mood worrying about Daddy. Instead I buckled down and spent the rest of the afternoon finishing the Tip Top radio spots.

After which I treated myself to a nice long soak in the tub, whiling away the time with some X-rated Justin fantasies.

My muscles limp as linguini, I climbed back into my pajamas (yes, I'd been wearing them all day—absolute heaven and one of the perks of being a freelance writer) and ordered Chinese takeout for dinner.

It showed up in no time, and I was just about to dig into my shrimp with lobster sauce when the phone rang.

Cue the storm clouds. It was Bebe.

I groaned inwardly at the sound of her voice.

"Anna's finished the alterations on your outfits," she said, "and I need you to come over to my studio right now to try them on."

"Now?"

Grrr! How aggravating! Just as I was about to eat.

"Yes, now. I need to make sure the clothes fit before the photo shoot."

I eyed my shrimp with lobster sauce longingly. Parting was such sweet sorrow!

What a ghastly end to a perfectly lovely day.

I slammed down the phone and shoved some shrimp in my mouth, little realizing just how ghastly things were about to get.

Chapter 10

I showed up at Casa Bebe, as instructed, surprised to find the picket gate out front wide open.

L.A.'s ubiquitous evening fog had rolled in, and the air was nippy. I hurried to the front door, wishing I'd worn a jacket over the sweats I'd hurriedly thrown on after Bebe's call.

I rang the bell several times, but there was no answer, so I started around the side of the house.

Out back, I saw that the French doors to Bebe's studio were flung wide open. How odd—with all this fog rolling in. Even odder, when I reached the studio, I saw Bebe slumped over her desk, her blond extensions splayed out around her.

Was it possible she was napping?

"Hi, Bebe," I called out.

No response.

I hesitated to wake her, afraid of erupting Mount Bebe. But I couldn't stand there all night, not when I had a carton of shrimp with lobster sauce waiting for me at home.

I crossed over to her desk, breathing in the scent of her Pine-Sol perfume.

And, for the first time, I noticed something stiff and metal poking out from Bebe's hair at the back of her neck.

This did not look good. Not good at all.

With a sinking sensation in my tummy, I pulled Bebe's hair apart and gasped to see a wire wound tight around her neck. Omigod! She'd been strangled—with one of her detested wire hangers!

It was then that I thought I heard a strange chirping noise coming from Bebe.

What if she was still alive? As much as I disliked the woman, I couldn't let her die.

So I frantically began untangling the wire from her neck.

"Bebe!" I shrieked once I'd loosened it. "Are you okay?"

The only response I got was the chirping noise. Which I now realized was coming from a cricket. I'd been in such a panic, I'd assumed it was Bebe.

But, no. Her body was still as a tomb, no signs of breathing.

She was gone, after all.

With trembling hands, I got out my cell phone and called 911.

It didn't take long for the police to show up.

And when they did, it suddenly occurred to me that I was standing at the scene of a crime with my fingerprints all over the murder weapon.

I warned you this day would not end well.

Was I right, or was I right?

Why, oh, why had I touched that damn wire hanger? And how on earth had I mistaken a cricket for Bebe?

What if the police found out how Bebe had used me as target practice for her insults? Or how I'd gleefully thrown darts at her poster? What if they thought that, sick of being humiliated, I'd snapped and killed her in a murderous rage?

Those were the fears swirling around my brain as I stood shivering outside Bebe's studio, waiting for the detective investigating the case to show up. When he finally did, he turned out to be a no-nonsense African American guy, graying at the temples, his hooded eyes looking like they'd seen far too many things he'd rather forget.

"Detective Washington, LAPD Homicide," he said, by way of introduction.

He flashed me his ID, and I couldn't help noticing his first name was Denzel.

"Denzel Washington?" I said. "Loved you in *Training Day*, haha."

Not even a glimmer of a smile. So much for cozying up to the cops.

Denzel took down my statement, issuing me a stern lecture about never touching anything at the scene of the crime, no doubt miffed that I'd compromised their physical evidence.

"I was just trying to save Bebe," I offered lamely. "I thought I heard her making a noise, but it turned out to be a cricket."

"A cricket, huh?" he said, clearly filing me away in his mental Rolodex as a prize doofus.

He proceeded to ask me some very disconcerting questions about whether Bebe and I had been on good terms. I couldn't possibly tell them the truth, that I thought she was an utter nightmare, a despot in designer togs. So I yakked about how grateful I was for her generosity in giving me the makeover.

I tried to sound appreciative, but I could tell Denzel wasn't quite buying it.

"Here's my business card," he said, eying me suspi-

ciously, "just in case there's something else you decide
you'd like to tell me."

Then he let me go with a warning not to leave town.

Never a good sign.

As you can imagine, I was more than a tad frazzled by
the whole experience, and the last thing I needed was
Lance bursting into my apartment the next morning before work, blathering about Bebe's murder.

"I can't believe it!" he cried. "Strangled with a wire
hanger! It's a Mommie Dearest Murder! . . . Mmm, yummy!"

That last part said as he snatched up a donut I'd been
about to eat.

"Apparently one of her clients found her. I wonder who
it was."

"Me," I sighed, slumping down onto my sofa, reliving
the whole miserable experience.

"You? I swear, Jaine, if you find one more dead body,
you can open your own cemetery."

Prozac looked up from where she'd been busy clawing
one of my throw pillows.

*If she'd been home with me, ministering to my every
need, this never would have happened.*

"What's worse," I moaned, "my fingerprints are all
over the murder weapon."

"How did that happen?" Lance asked, dunking his purloined donut into my coffee.

I told him everything.

"Ouch!" he said when I was through. "That's awful!
But you've got to look on the bright side."

"Which is?"

"Prozac's video has more than five thousand views!"

A triumphant meow from Prozac.

I'm a star! Quick! Somebody buy me a limo!

"And besides," Lance said, "you've got nothing to worry about. I know who the killer is."

"You do?"

"Sure, it's Sven Gustafson."

"Who the heck is Sven Gustafson?"

"I told you about him. He works with me at Neiman's. Bebe used to be his customer until she dumped him for me. He's resented her ever since. And he called in sick three days last week. Probably home plotting the murder. I've already reported him to the police hotline."

"And what did they say?"

"That yes, they'd look into it and no, that they weren't interested in Neiman's half-yearly sale on Ferragamos."

With that, he polished off my donut and headed for the door.

"Ciao for now, sweetheart. You know I love you to pieces!"

Needless to say, he was talking to Prozac.

Chapter 11

Haunted by the specter of my fingerprints on Bebe's murder weapon, and afraid that any minute now I'd be hauled off to police headquarters in handcuffs, I decided to put on my detective shoes and do a little snooping.

(I don't like to brag, but I've solved more than my fair share of homicides in my day, stirring sagas of murder, mayhem, and runaway calories you can read about in the titles listed at the front of this book.)

So when I saw an announcement of Bebe's funeral in the paper, I made up my mind to be there.

The funeral was being held at Westwood Mortuary, cemetery to the stars, the final resting place of legends like Marilyn Monroe, Natalie Wood, and Kirk Douglas. Also, not quite so legendary, Rodney Dangerfield, whose epitaph reads "There goes the neighborhood."

Lance took time off from work to join me, unwilling to miss any celebrity sightings.

And indeed there were some A-listers in the crowd, along with a cadre of stick-thin socialites and two Real Housewives of Beverly Hills.

(I only hoped The Housewives wouldn't wind up bashing each other with Bebe's funeral wreath.)

Among the celebs was Lacey Hunt, Bebe's pilfered

client, looking fresh-faced and rosy-cheeked in funereal black. She wore a sorrowful expression, eyes misted with tears, but somehow I got the feeling that I was watching a performance, something she'd learned in Acting 101. (Especially when I saw her taking sneak peeks at her cell phone.)

Miles was there, too, the bereaved husband, looking appropriately mournful, his beefy body crammed into his suit. And over at the edge of the crowd was Tatiana, Bebe's former mentor and rival stylist, her jet-black hair cemented in place, bright red lipstick bleeding into her lip lines, wearing the same frayed outfit she'd worn the day she came storming into Bebe's studio. I couldn't help but notice a faint smile on those ruby lips as she sidled over to Lacey Hunt and whispered in her ear, no doubt eager to woo back her former client.

I remembered how furious she'd been the day she came barging into Bebe's studio, threatening to get revenge on Bebe for poaching Lacey.

Now I wondered if she'd made good on her threat and strangled her detested rival.

I scanned the crowd for Heidi and Justin (especially Justin), but neither of them was there. Can't say I blamed them; they'd probably had more than their fill of Bebe while she was alive.

The only employee who showed up was Anna, the seamstress, looking mousy as ever in an inexpensive black dress, her pale face partially obscured by a curtain of lanky brown hair. Frankly, I was surprised to see her, given how badly Bebe had treated her.

As the minister spun a fairy tale about what a warm, loving person Bebe had been, Lance recognized several of his customers among the mourners and began whispering a running commentary about their foot ailments:

"There's Buffy Cohen. Bunions the size of golf balls."

"Mitzi Doheny. Belongs in the Hammertoe Hall of Fame."

"And Camilla Von Durst. All her millions, and she can't get rid of her toenail fungus."

Clearly I was not the only one who could hear Lance's whispers.

At one point, the minister looked up from his pack of lies to shoot Lance a dirty look. Which silenced him, but only for a minute or so.

"Omigod," he whispered as a slim, blond fashion plate of a guy came walking across the graveyard to join the mourners. "That's Sven Gustafson! Bebe's killer! Check out the sneaky look on his face."

I checked out Sven's face, bland and handsome, not the least bit sneaky.

It was hard to picture him as a killer, even harder when his only motive seemed to have been that Bebe dropped him as her shoe salesman.

"I can't believe he had the nerve to show up," Lance fumed. "Probably a ruse to throw the cops off his trail."

I'm happy to report that, when the service was over, no funeral wreaths had been tossed by scene-stealing house-wives. As the crowd started to disperse, Lance dashed over to schmooze with his customers while I made a much-needed trip to the chapel ladies' room.

(I really must stop drinking so much coffee in the morning. But I need something to wash down my cinnamon raisin bagels, don't I?)

The chapel was deserted when I got there, my footsteps echoing down the corridor.

I made use of the facilities, enjoying the luxury of washing my hands with lily-scented soap and drying them on a paper towel as thick as terry cloth. The rich sure knew how to pamper their mourners in style.

I was just about to leave when I heard someone talking in the deserted corridor. I recognized the voice. It was Miles.

"See, babe?" he was saying. "I told you everything would work out."

Babe? Who was he calling *babe?*

"But we can't be seen together for a while. The police will suspect us if they know about our affair."

Holy moly. Miles was having an affair! Talk about your motives for murder.

I opened the door a crack, hoping to see the object of his affections.

And sure enough, I did.

There in the hallway, Miles was kissing shy little Anna, the seamstress! Only she didn't look the least bit shy now, her lips locked on Miles.

In the wake of Bebe's death, these two were happy campers.

Very happy campers, indeed.

I stared at them, mesmerized, not sure if I was watching an adulterous couple—or an adulterous couple of killers.

Chapter 12

After witnessing that steamy smoochfest between Miles and Anna, I made up my mind to have a chat with the grieving widower.

So the next day, armed with the ultimate comfort food—some creamy macaroni and cheese I'd picked up at the supermarket—I showed up at Casa Bebe under the guise of paying a condolence call.

As I made my way up the path to the front door, past the battalion of security signs warning of hidden cameras and armed guard responses, I was struck by a glorious thought: surely one of the many security cameras had captured a picture of the killer. Murder solved, just like that!

Unless, of course, the killer had managed to disarm the cameras. Someone who had access to the security system, someone who actually lived in the house with Bebe—namely, Miles.

When I rang the bell, he came to the door, looking pretty darn chipper for a guy who'd just lost his wife—standing tall, eyes bright, a smile on his lips. Then, just a beat too late, he lost the smile and tried his best to look like a husband in mourning.

"Hey, Jaine."

Not exactly thrilled to see me. But that didn't stop me from turning on the charm.

"I'm sorry I didn't have a chance to talk to you at the funeral, so I came to pay my respects."

"Thanks," he said, showing no signs of inviting me in.

"I brought you macaroni and cheese," I offered, hoping this would soften him up.

It did not.

"Great," he said, grabbing it and starting to close the door.

But he wasn't about to get rid of me. Not that easily.

"It's the least I could do," I said, skittering past him into the house. "After all, you were so kind to me that day I first came to see Bebe, feeding me tea and brownies. It was very sweet of you."

And it was. But I couldn't concentrate on his good side, not when I was trying to convict him of murder.

"I can't stay long," I said, making a beeline for the living room, where I plopped myself firmly down onto a massive white sofa.

Reluctantly, Miles joined me, taking a seat in a nearby armchair.

Across from us, over a gray slate fireplace, was a framed poster of Bebe, a larger version of the one I'd seen in Heidi's office.

"Such a tragedy about Bebe," I murmured.

"Indeed," he nodded stiffly.

"I guess the police already know who the killer is."

"Last I heard, they thought it was you."

"Wait, no! It wasn't me, I swear. I just came by for a fitting and happened to be the one who found her body. What about all your security cameras? Don't they show footage of the killer?"

He took a break from his grieving widower act to laugh out loud.

"Hah. There are no cameras. Bebe was way too cheap to spring for a security system. All she bought were the signs."

"No cameras?"

"Nope. Not a one."

Which meant I was still alive and well on the cops' suspect list.

"Can I get you a plate for that?" Miles asked.

I looked down and saw that, in my state of mini-panic, I'd opened the container of mac and cheese and was digging into it with a plastic take-out fork.

Gaak! How embarrassing.

"I'm so sorry!" I cried. "This is for you, not me."

"Go for it," he said with a wave of his hand. "I've got plenty of food."

"I couldn't possibly," I said, snapping the lid back on the container.

"So how are you holding up?" I asked, with my best condolence call smile.

"It's been tough," he replied, with his best grieving widower sigh. "Bebe and I were together since high school."

He picked up a photo from an end table and handed it to me.

I gazed down at Miles, looking impossibly young and buff in a football uniform, his arm slung around a teenage Bebe, reed thin in a cheerleader's outfit, smiling a gap-toothed smile that had long since been corrected by cosmetic dentistry.

"I fell for Bebe the first time I saw her," Miles said, "walking across campus like a model in a fashion magazine. She made all the other girls look like country bumpkins. I knew right away she was someone special."

From the wistful look in in his eyes, I could tell this was no act. He'd really been in love with that long ago version of Bebe.

"I was the famous one back then, playing varsity football, with an athletic scholarship to UCLA. I planned on going pro, but that went south when I busted my knee in my senior year."

He shook his head, still pained at the memory.

"It all worked out in the end, though," he said, snapping out of his reverie. "I wound up working with Bebe in the fashion industry, which has been very rewarding."

Oh, please. Not for one minute did I believe that working for Bebe as her lackey had been the least bit rewarding. Stripped of his dignity, toting clothes to and from the dry cleaners, he must've hated every bit of it.

Add the fact that he had a girlfriend on the side and probably stood to inherit a bundle, he had more than enough motive to kill Bebe.

Miles may have put on a few pounds since his glory days, but as an ex-footballer, he certainly had the strength to wring that wire hanger around Bebe's neck.

"If only I'd been home that night," he was saying, "I might've seen the killer and stopped him.

"Or *her*," he added, shooting me a look much like the one lobbed at me by Detective Denzel Washington.

"But unfortunately, I was at my cigar lounge."

"Cigar lounge?"

"Bebe never let me smoke cigars in the house. She hated the smell. So I went to the El Dorado Cigar Lounge in Brentwood. I was there all night watching the Laker's game."

Darn it all. It looked like he had an alibi.

I desperately needed some time alone to dig for dirt on this guy.

"Gosh," I said, "I hate to ask in your time of mourning, but I don't suppose I could have the makeover outfits Bebe chose for me? They were so gorgeous."

"No problem. I'm going to be liquidating all the stuff in the studio anyway."

So much for his avid devotion to the fashion industry.

"Wait here," he said. "I'll be right back."

The minute he left, I got up and started snooping.

I didn't know what I expected to discover, but it never hurt to look.

Right away, I hit the jackpot when I opened an end table drawer and found a picture of Anna tucked in a travel brochure for Bali—perhaps a "We Got Away with Murder" vacation for the lovebirds once the investigation wrapped up and some innocent person—namely *moi*—was festering behind bars for a crime she didn't commit.

I was so upset at the thought of me sharing a jail cell with a gal named Duke, I could hardly swallow my mac and cheese.

(What can I say? Snooping makes me hungry.)

Then I wandered over to the fireplace, where Bebe still lived in her poster, forever stylish behind the glass of the frame.

In the sunlight streaming in from the room's large picture windows, I noticed what looked like small circles dotting the glass. How odd. Then I realized they were the same kind of circles left by the suction darts Heidi and I had been hurling at Bebe's poster that day in her office.

Had Miles been taking shots at his wife when she wasn't around? And then, not content with lashing out at her image, had he taken out his wrath in real life?

I was mulling over this thought and polishing off the last of the mac and cheese when Miles returned with two dresses, a pair of slacks, and that blue cashmere sweater I'd been lusting after.

All of which were on wire hangers.

A declaration of freedom if I ever saw one.

And once more I wondered if Miles had used what was left of his athletic prowess to wring the life out of his bitch of a wife.

Chapter 13

There may be some chocolate-flavored cereal lovers out there who are right now asking themselves: "Whatever happened to Jaine's CUCKOO FOR COCOA PUFFS T-shirt? And why the heck isn't she trying to find it?"

Let me assure you I had not forgotten about my beloved tee. In fact, as soon as Justin texted me Felipe the gardener's contact info, I'd lined up an appointment to see him and was scheduled to show up at his house in East L.A. that very night.

In the meanwhile, however, I still had to deal with the repercussions from Prozac's video.

Trevor's mom, Trudy (by now, we were on a first name basis), had been on a buying spree, bombarding Pro with a boatload of gifts—including a plush canopy bed that Pro was using as a litter box, and a towering cat tree from which my fractious furball dive-bombed my head every time I walked by.

Trudy also sent over a yummy looking Thank You cake, which I naturally assumed was for me, until I saw the Kitty Katz Bakery label on the box. Turns out it was made out of tuna, and actually, it wasn't that bad.

(Okay, so I had a taste. Sue me.)

Yes, Pro was becoming quite the little celebrity, so I

shouldn't have been surprised when that afternoon I got a call from a *Los Angeles Times* reporter, requesting an interview.

I would have turned her down flat had she not mentioned that the paper wanted to run a picture of me and Prozac along with the interview. Which meant I'd get a chance to counteract the image of my giant tush in cyberspace. I'd wear a spiffy new outfit, maybe my new blue cashmere sweater, and be photographed with my tush facing away—far away—from the camera.

Not ten minutes after agreeing to do the interview, I got another call—this time from a gal named Matilda at a pet charity called Paws Across America, inviting Prozac to be the guest of honor at their annual gala dinner.

The interview was one thing, but no way was Prozac about to get any more adulation for a heroic deed she never performed.

"I'm sorry," I said to Matilda, "but we won't be able to attend."

"Oh, that's too bad. We've invited your local councilman to give Prozac a kibble key to the city."

"It sounds lovely, but I'm afraid not."

"And it's a really special event, a steak dinner at the Beverly Hilton."

Whoa, Nelly!

"Steak dinner, huh?"

"Prime sirloin."

"Um. Let me check my calendar." I held the phone for a few beats pretending to check my fictional calendar. "Yes, I think we can make it after all."

And so I had agreed to not one, but *two* events honoring a cat who was in fact at that very moment pooping in her canopy bed.

*   *   *

After a mind-numbing slog on the 10 freeway, nearby snails giggling as they whizzed past me, I finally showed up at Felipe's home in East L.A.

In the light of the setting sun, I saw a neat, well-kept bungalow, with clusters of yellow roses peeking through a white picket fence, the path to his house lined with bright pink impatiens and velvety pansies.

Clearly the home of a gardener.

Felipe came to the door, a fiftysomething man with a thick thatch of salt-and-pepper hair. Over jeans and a white T-shirt, he wore a distinctly un-macho floral apron.

My first impression of him was pretty fuzzy, however, distracted as I was by the smell of something yummy cooking in his kitchen.

"How can I help you?" he asked.

Feed me! was what I felt like saying, salivating at the heavenly aroma.

But I wrenched myself back to the reason for my visit.

"I'm Jaine Austen. We met at Bebe Braddock's house. I was there to get a makeover."

"Right. The lady with the CUCKOO FOR COCOA PUFFS T-shirt."

"Justin told me you were holding it for me."

"Yes, I was."

Was? Past tense? Don't tell me he'd let my precious tee slip through his fingers!

"But then my niece Gloria stopped by for dinner one night and said she had to have it."

Obviously a gal of impeccable taste.

"She wanted to wear it with a tinfoil hat to get out of jury duty."

Of all the nerve!

"I'm certain she's still got it," Felipe assured me. "Let me write down her address."

As he hurried back into his house, I stepped inside Felipe's cozy living room, taking deep breaths of whatever was cooking in the kitchen. Minutes later, Felipe returned with his niece's address.

"Thanks so much," I said as he handed it to me.

Now at that point, any person with an inkling of good manners would have vamoosed.

But, as you already know, when it comes to chow, I have no shame whatsoever. So I did not vamoose.

Instead I said, "Gee, it sure smells good in here."

"I was just fixing myself dinner. Carne asada, with rice and beans. Albondigas soup to start."

"Albondigas soup? It's my favorite!"

I did not lie. If you've never had some, try it ipso pronto. Miniature meatballs swimming in a rich broth studded with chopped veggies. And don't even get me started on carne asada with black beans and rice.

"Come!" he said, as I stood there, my feet practically having grown roots in his carpet. "Join me!"

"I couldn't possibly," I said, hot on his heels as he led the way to his kitchen.

Minutes later, we were seated at his Formica-topped kitchen table, slurping albondigas soup.

"Wow, this is fantastic!" I said between slurps.

"It's my grandmother's recipe. I used to make it for my wife all the time before she passed."

His face clouded over.

"I'm so sorry for your loss," I said, wanting to reach out and pat his hand in sympathy.

But no way was I about to let go of my soup spoon.

"It's been ten years," he sighed, "and I still expect to see her walking through the front door."

Unlike Miles, Felipe seemed like a guy who genuinely missed his spouse.

"I cooked for her all the time," he said as he brought me a plate heaped with carne asada, beans, and rice.

"Lucky lady!" I said, digging into the most heavenly carne asada north of Guadalajara.

"I'm glad you stopped by," Felipe said, watching me eat. "I like to see a woman with a hearty appetite. Ladies today," he tsked, "are too skinny."

I was growing fonder of this guy by the minute.

"Like Mrs. Braddock." He shook his head in disapproval. "Skinny as a rail."

"I still can't believe somebody killed her," I said.

"I can. I don't like to speak ill of the departed, but Mrs. Braddock was not a nice woman. Nobody liked her."

Hello. It looked like Felipe was about to dish the dirt.

"I bet she was tough to work for," I said, egging him on.

"The worst. Always expecting me to do extra jobs, never offering to pay for my time. She took advantage of me, just like she took advantage of everyone. The only people she was nice to were her movie-star clients. The rest of us? We were nothing but peasants to her."

"That's awful," I said, sopping up my black beans with a tortilla.

"The way she treated her husband was a disgrace. Bossing him around like a servant. And poor Anna, such a sweet lady. Mrs. Braddock was terrible to her. It's hard to believe she could be so mean to her own sister."

Wait, what? Stop the presses.

"Anna was Bebe's sister?"

"Unfortunately for Anna, yes."

Holy moly! Felipe had just fed me the juiciest tidbit of all. Suffering abuse is one thing. But from your sister? I could only imagine how Anna must have resented Bebe. Maybe even enough to kill her. Especially if she stood to inherit money in Bebe's will.

A gazillion calories later, after thanking Felipe for one of the best meals of my life, I returned to my Corolla, armed with a shiny new motive for Anna to have killed Bebe, and—even more important—a container of Felipe's amazing albondigas soup tucked in my tote.

Chapter 14

Okay, so Anna had plenty of reasons to kill Bebe.

But did she actually do it? Or had she let her muscle-bound lover do the job for her? Maybe it was Miles who wrangled the wire around Bebe's neck, with Anna cheering him on from the sidelines.

Those of you paying close attention to my little story will no doubt remember Miles telling me he'd been smoking stogies at the El Dorado Cigar Lounge at the time of the murder.

And so I decided to stop by that establishment on my way home from Felipe's.

I found it in the heart of Brentwood, nestled between a Pilates studio and a gluten-free pizza parlor (only in L.A.!).

Unlike its froufrou neighbors, the lounge was a dim, dark man cave of a joint, furnished with plush leather wing chairs. A glass sales counter on one side of the store faced a massive flat-screen TV mounted on the opposite wall. Several men were scattered about, puffing on cigars and watching a basketball game, when I showed up.

But what I noticed most when I walked in the door was the ghastly stench of cigars. Frankly, I didn't blame Bebe for making Miles smoke his stinkbombs outside the house.

I headed over to the man behind the sales counter, a middle-aged guy in a black silk shirt, his graying hair in a ponytail.

He looked me up and down, skeptically.

"Are you sure you're in the right place?" he asked, his eyes lingering just a beat too long on my hips. "You're not looking for gluten-free pizza next door?"

Clearly Mr. El Dorado and I were not destined to be BFFs.

"No," I said, forcing myself to smile, "I'm here to buy a cigar. Miles Braddock recommended your lounge very highly."

"Miles!" he said, a tad friendlier. "One of my best customers."

"A real tragedy about his wife, huh?"

"I can't get over it," he shuddered. "Garroted with a hanger."

"Poor Miles. He said if only he'd been home that night and not here at your cigar lounge, he might have been able to stop the killer. He was here that night, right?"

"Yep, sitting right over there." Mr. El Dorado pointed to a wing chair near the store's entrance. "He was there all night watching a Lakers game. Came in at seven, didn't go home until after ten."

There was something about the way he said this, a tad too rehearsed, that made me wonder if Miles had paid him to back up his alibi.

"So what can I get you?" he asked, gesturing to a display of cigars in the glass counter. All of which looked pretty much the same to me.

"I'll smoke what Miles smokes."

"Excellent choice! Robust flavor!"

He took out a burrito-sized cigar from the case.

"That'll be fifty dollars."

Holy Moses!

"On second thought, maybe I'll try something a little less robust."

"How much less robust?"

"Forty bucks less."

"Here's a nice one for only eighteen dollars."

Eighteen bucks for a stinky cigar?!

Reluctantly I handed him my Mastercard.

"Anything else?" He gestured to a display of cigar accessories.

"No, I'm set," I said, refusing to fork over one more dime to this guy.

He gave me my cigar, wrapped in cellophane, and I made my way to Miles's chair near the entrance.

When I plopped my fanny down into the well-worn leather, I was disappointed to see there was nothing blocking the view from the cigar counter. Maybe Mr. El Dorado really did see Miles parked in this chair from seven to ten PM.

A part of me wanted to throw in the towel and flee from the noxious cigar fumes. But another part of me was telling me to stick around. There was something about Mr. El Dorado that I just didn't trust.

I couldn't very well sit in a cigar lounge without smoking a cigar, so I decided to go ahead and smoke the darn thing. I mean, how difficult could it be?

As it turned out, very-to-impossible.

For starters, how was I going to light it?

"Excuse me," I said to a bearded guy bent over a laptop, banging out what was probably a screenplay. "Do you have any matches? I forgot to bring mine."

"Sure," he said, handing me a box.

"You might want to take off that cellophane wrapper first," he warned as I started to strike a match.

Duh. Mistake Number One.

I removed the wrapper and crumpled it into a nearby ashtray.

Once again, I was about to strike the match when my bearded buddy asked: "Aren't you going to cut it first?"

Cut it?

"Here. You can use my cutter."

He handed me a stainless steel doohickey that looked like a miniature guillotine. I had absolutely no idea what to do with it.

"Let me," he said, taking the cutter and expertly snipping off the end of my cigar.

"Thanks so much," I said, beaming him a grateful smile.

"No!" he cried as I put the cigar in my mouth. "Wrong end. The other end goes into your mouth."

Mistake Number Two.

With the right end of the cigar in my mouth, I struck a match and after a strenuous couple of puffs, the cigar finally ignited.

At last! I was about to smoke my very first cigar.

But then I made Mistake Number Three. And it was a doozy.

I inhaled.

Yikes! That thing burned. My throat felt like scorched sandpaper. How was I supposed to know you're supposed to puff a cigar, not inhale it?

After a minor coughing fit, I set the cigar down in the ashtray and began rummaging in my tote for a mint to soothe my aching throat.

By now my screenwriter friend had abandoned his laptop, watching me, fascinated, no doubt preserving this scene to use somewhere in his movie. I certainly hoped he thanked me when and if he ever won an Oscar.

I finally found a mint wedged under the container of Felipe's albondigas soup I'd stowed in my tote.

I was sitting there, sucking on the mint and listening to the raucous cheers of the men watching the basketball game when suddenly I smelled something burning.

"I think your ashtray's on fire," my bearded buddy was kind enough to point out.

Oh, hell. I turned and saw flames leaping from my ashtray. Damn it all. The cellophane from my cigar had caught fire!

How the heck was I going to put it out?

I looked around frantically. A guy nearby was drinking what looked like scotch, but I didn't dare throw alcohol on a burning fire.

You know where this is going, right? As much as I hated to do it, I had to use Felipe's albondigas soup.

I yanked it out of my tote bag and pried open the lid of the container, and before you could say "Ay, caramba!" I was dousing the fire with albondigas soup.

I watched, brokenhearted, as one of Felipe's yummy meatballs floated in the ashtray.

All very embarrassing, to be sure.

But here's something I think you'll find interesting. I know I did.

While I'd been setting my ashtray on fire, somebody on the Lakers had scored a free throw. Cheers erupted from the men. No one aside from the screenwriter had noticed that I'd almost burned down the building.

Including, and especially, Mr. El Dorado.

And at that moment, Miles' alibi went flying out the window.

He could have come and gone from the cigar lounge on the night of the murder, killing half of L.A., and Mr. El Dorado would have never noticed.

Chapter 15

Now that I'd busted Miles's alibi, it was time to check up on his lover and possible partner in crime, Anna.

Unfortunately I had no idea how to reach her. In fact, I didn't even know her last name. When I got up the next morning, I thought about calling Justin and asking him to send me a link to Bebe's contacts, but I hesitated to make the call.

I hadn't heard from him since our last date. Not a word about that violin recital he'd invited me to. According to my calendar, it was supposed to happen that very night. Maybe he found out about my fingerprints on the murder weapon. Some men (say, 99.9 percent) might find that a bit of a turnoff.

But I really wanted to talk to Anna. So, gathering my courage, I put in a call to Justin, hoping he hadn't heard about me being at the scene of the crime.

Alas, I hoped in vain.

"Jaine!" he cried when he picked up. "What happened? Miles told me the police found you standing over Bebe's dead body with your fingerprints all over the murder weapon."

Thank you, Miles "Blabbermouth" Braddock.

"It's all a horrible misunderstanding! I swear, I had nothing to do with Bebe's murder."

"Of course not."

Uh-oh. Was that a hint of doubt I heard in his voice?

"Anyhow, I was hoping you could send me a link to Bebe's contact list so I can nose around and question a few people."

"You mean, like a private investigator?"

"Kinda sorta."

"Writer *and* private eye, huh? How intriguing."

Still, that note of doubt in his voice.

"By the way," he said, "about that violin recital I invited you to tonight? There's been a change of plans."

What did I tell you? He was about to bail. I knew he'd be one of the 99.9 percent of guys who steered clear of dating murder suspects.

"It's going to start at 7:00 instead of 7:30. So I'll pick you up around six."

"You still want to go out with me?"

"Of course. You didn't think I was going to cancel just because of that fingerprints-on-the-murder-weapon thing, did you?"

"The thought had crossed my mind."

"Don't be nuts. I know you didn't kill Bebe. You're much too nice."

Did you hear that? In addition to being a cutie pie musical prodigy, Justin was also a discerning judge of character!

I hung up in a happy glow, eager to see him in action tonight.

(And to hear him play his violin, too.)

*   *   *

Minutes later, Justin texted me a link to Bebe's contacts.

My plan was to hotfoot it to Anna, but then I saw Heidi's name on the list. I hadn't forgotten the great haircut she'd picked out for me. If I popped by and visited her today, maybe she could style my hair for my date with Justin.

My visit to Anna would have to wait.

I just hoped Heidi hadn't started that studio job she'd been offered. But she was home when I texted her and said she'd be happy to see me and cut my hair.

I tootled over to her apartment, the upstairs unit of a charming Spanish duplex in the mid-Wilshire area of Los Angeles.

Heidi greeted me at the door in overalls and a T-shirt, her glossy hair swept back in a bandana headband.

"Jaine! It's so good to see you!" she said, ushering me into her apartment, a cozy nest that hadn't been updated since flappers were doing the Charleston. All the wonderful architectural details were still intact—hardwood floors, arched doorways, and crystal glass doorknobs.

In her living room, a pink velvet sofa sat center stage, adorned by palm-frond throw pillows and surrounded by vintage rattan furniture. All set off by walls painted a bright lime green.

If I tried doing that stuff, I'd be arrested by the Decorating Police. But somehow Heidi managed to pull it off.

"I can't wait to get my hands on your hair," she said.

"Are you sure it's not a bother?"

"Not at all. I don't start my studio job until next week, so I've had plenty of time to cut my private clients' hair."

Suddenly I wondered how much she charged those private clients.

"Do you mind telling me your fee?"

"Usually two hundred dollars."

Wowser. I wanted to look good for Justin, but two hundred dollars was way out of my comfort zone.

"But today's cut is my treat," she grinned. "Consider it combat pay for having to put up with Bebe."

Was she an angel, or what?

"C'mon," she said, leading me past a tiny dining room to a sunlit kitchen gleaming with bright turquoise and yellow backsplash tiles.

"Welcome to my salon," she said. "Let's get your hair washed first."

Soon I was leaning over her kitchen sink with a towel draped around my neck as Heidi washed my hair with a heavenly citrus-scented shampoo—followed by an equally heavenly citrus-scented conditioner.

Then she sat me down at her kitchen table and took a pair of scissors from one of her overall pockets.

"I know we decided on beachy waves for your makeover," she said. "Bebe hated curly hair. But I think you'd really look better with your natural curls. Do you mind if I give it a shot?"

"Shoot away!"

"So," she said as she started snipping, "how are you holding up?"

"Holding up?"

"I mean, after the police found you with your fingerprints on the murder weapon."

"You know about that?"

"Miles happened to mention it."

Boy, Miles sure was tossing around that tidbit of info, wasn't he?

"When I discovered Bebe's body, I wasn't sure if she was still alive," I said, "so I tried to loosen the wire hanger from around her neck. That's why my fingerprints were on the murder weapon."

"You actually tried to save her? Talk about no good deed going unpunished."

"I don't suppose you have any idea who might have killed her?"

"Just about anybody whoever had to deal with her. The possibilities are endless."

"Did you know that Miles and Anna were having an affair?" I asked, zeroing in on my two favorite suspects.

"No!" she said, wide-eyed. "I figured Miles might be cheating on Bebe. After all, she was such a holy terror. But I never dreamed it was with mousy little Anna."

"Who just happens to be Bebe's sister."

"I knew about that. And I hated the way Bebe treated her. Well, Anna sure got her revenge sleeping with Miles, didn't she?"

Maybe even the ultimate revenge: Murder.

"Do you think Anna might have built up enough resentment over the years to have killed Bebe?" I asked.

"She's such a timid little thing, it's hard to believe, but then I'd never believe she was boffing Miles, so anything's possible. Like I said, Bebe had so many enemies, anyone could have done it."

Heidi was right. Anyone could have done it. Including, I hated to admit, Heidi herself.

It didn't seem very likely. But I couldn't afford to rule anyone out.

"If only I hadn't shown up at the studio the night of the murder," I said.

"Talk about bad timing," Heidi agreed.

"Where were you that night?" I asked, as casually as possible. "Far from Brentwood, I hope."

"I was here at the apartment, working on my sculpture."

"Your sculpture?"

"Yes, it's a hobby of mine. I love to make things out of found objects. I troll the trash on garbage days, looking for stuff to work with. It's been a wonderful creative outlet, the only thing that kept me sane working for Bebe."

She proceeded to tell me about her latest project—a giraffe made from vacuum cleaner parts—as she snipped away at my hair.

When she'd snipped her last snip, she plugged in a diffuser and started shaping my curls.

Then she stepped back and looked me over.

"I love it!" she cried, grinning. "Let's go look in the mirror."

With that, she led me down a narrow hallway to her bathroom, a cluttered affair with a claw-foot tub and blouses drying from her shower rod.

I checked myself out in her medicine cabinet mirror and loved what I saw—a nimbus of glorious curls that framed my face to perfection.

"Heidi, I adore it! Are you sure I can't pay you something?"

"Absolutely not. It's my pleasure."

No way could this darling woman possibly be a killer.

"C'mon," she said, taking my hand, "I want to show you my giraffe."

We crossed the narrow hallway to the bedroom she used as her studio.

"What do you think?" she asked, showing me an ingenious configuration of vacuum cleaner parts.

"Wow," I said, gobsmacked.

But my eyes had strayed from the giraffe to a sculpture in the corner of the room.

Another animal. This time, a horse. And not just any horse. This one had been made entirely out of—wait for it—wire hangers.

Heidi may not have seemed like a killer, but she sure had plenty of experience working with the murder weapon.

Chapter 16

I drove home, more than a tad discombobulated by the sight of Heidi's wire-hanger horse. Heidi was a darling woman and fantastic hairstylist, but, as much as it pained me, I had to add her to my suspect list. With Bebe gone, Heidi was free to accept the lucrative studio job she'd been lusting after.

All thoughts of Heidi went flying out the window, however, when I returned home and stepped into my living room.

The place was a shambles.

I gasped to see books knocked down from my bookcase, my African violet overturned, seat cushions upended, and throw pillows strewn all over the room.

For a frightening instant, I thought I'd been burglarized.

But then I saw the culprit—my pampered princess snoring on the sofa, her catnip mouse in tatters on the floor below.

No, I hadn't been robbed. Just hit by Hurricane Prozac.

"Prozac Elizabeth Austen!" I cried. "Look at this god-awful mess you've made!"

She opened a sleepy eye and purred proudly.

Impressive, isn't it?

Then she rolled over and resumed her beauty rest, her

snores as loud as my curses as I stomped around, putting books back up on the shelf, vacuuming spilled dirt from my African violet, and returning throw pillows to their rightful places. Not to mention picking up the trash from the knocked-over garbage bin in my kitchen.

When all had been restored to order, I fixed myself a dietetic lunch of Wheat Thins and chunk white tuna (filched from Trudy's gift stash for Prozac).

It wasn't exactly a Quarter Pounder, but it would have to do. I wanted to stay as svelte as possible for my date with Justin that night.

Just as I was scraping the last shards of tuna from my plate, the phone rang. It was the gang from Tip Top, with some changes for the "Drop Your Pants" radio spots. It wasn't much, just a few tweaks. I should have been able to churn it out in an hour, tops.

But when I sat down at my computer, with a few extra Wheat Thins for sustenance, I found myself struggling to keep my eyes open.

Ever since this whole Cat Who Saved a Toddler's Life thing began, Prozac had been in flaming diva mode, hogging my pillow, draping her tail over my nose, and putting a serious damper on my quality sleep time. That, plus all the energy I'd spent cleaning up in the wake of her catnip rampage, had left me wiped out.

I struggled to peck out a few sentences on my keyboard, but it was no use. I simply couldn't keep my eyes open.

So I put my head down on the table to rest.

My, that felt good. All I needed was a few minutes, and I'd be up and running.

Yeah, right.

The next thing I knew, I was being jarred out of a deep sleep by a loud knocking at my front door.

I checked the time: Six o'clock.

Omigosh, it was Justin, and I hadn't had a chance to change my outfit. What's more, I had sleep crud in my eyes and tuna on my breath. A fact confirmed by Prozac, who was sniffing my face, clearly peeved.

Hey, is that MY tuna I smell on your breath?

"Just a minute!" I called out, racing to the bathroom, where I splashed water on my face and swished my mouth with Listerine.

Then a mad dash to open the front door.

Justin, my boy toy dreamboat, was standing there all spiffed up for his violin recital, his hair slicked back, his dimple flashing. Underneath his TEAM BEBE bomber jacket, he wore a dress shirt and tie.

"Hey there," he said, shooting me a most endearing grin. "Ready to hear me put Itzhak Perlman to shame?"

"Almost. I'm afraid I fell asleep, and I haven't had a chance to change."

"No worries," he said, looking me up and down. "You look great."

And he seemed to mean it.

Brava! I was one of those women who could get away with elastic-waist jeans and no makeup!

"But what's that in your hair?" Frowning, he reached into my curls and pulled out something brown and crumbly. "Is this an Oreo?"

Okay, so I didn't have Wheat Thins with my tuna. I had Oreos. (You should have guessed as much.)

And Justin had just plucked a rather large chunk from my hair.

How mortifying.

Stuff like this happens to her all the time.

By now Prozac had scurried to Justin's side and was doing her pole dance routine around his ankles.

One time she woke up with a pretzel in her ear.

He bent down to pick her up.

"How are you, cute thing?"

Just fine, now that you're here. Whaddaya say you ditch the cookie monster and spend the next several hours scratching me behind my ears?

"That's enough out of you, young lady," I said, wrenching her from Justin's arms and plopping her down on the sofa. "Justin and I need to leave if we don't want to be late for his violin recital.

"Shall we?" I said to Justin, ignoring Prozac's yowls of protest and hustling him out the door.

Outside, I saw his motorcycle parked at the curb.

Fooey. I'd forgotten about those darn motorcycle helmets. So much for my fabulous Heidi do.

"So how are things going with your murder investigation?" Justin asked as we made our way down the front path. "Any suspects?"

"Plenty!" I told him about Anna and Miles's secret affair, Miles's bogus alibi, and Heidi's wire-hanger horse.

"Just so long as I'm not on your list," he said, flashing me his dimple.

"Of course not. Haha."

And then—like a bolt of lightning that should have struck me several chapters ago—I wondered: What if Justin was the killer? Up to that moment, I'd been so blinded by his Adorability Quotient, the thought hadn't even crossed my mind.

By now, we were at the curb. After strapping on our helmets and making sure Justin's violin was secure in his storage case, we climbed on board the cycle.

"Here we go!" he cried, taking off.

Riding along with my arms around Justin's waist, my body pressed up against his, I should have felt all sorts of tingling in my lady parts.

But my lady parts were distinctly tingle-free.

Instead all I felt was a growing sense of unease, wondering with every bump in the road if Justin had knocked off Queen Bebe.

True, of all her employees, Bebe seemed to treat Justin fairly well, and he'd seemed immune to her abuse. But who knew what secret resentments he might have been harboring? His nonchalance could be an act. Maybe he'd been seething inside over something awful Bebe had done to him, waiting for the right moment to wring a wire hanger around her neck.

I had to face facts.

For all I knew, I could be riding with my arms clutched around the world's most adorable killer.

Chapter 17

We rode over to the recital, me stewing all the way, hoping Justin wasn't the killer. I reminded myself that with Bebe dead, Justin was out of a job. Unlike Heidi, he had no new lucrative gig waiting in the wings. So he had every reason to want Bebe alive and well and signing his paychecks.

By the time we got to the parking lot of the middle school in Westwood where the recital was taking place, I was so lost in my thoughts, I barely noticed when I shook off my helmet and a few more Oreo crumbs came flying out of my hair.

"Wish me luck," Justin said, taking his violin from his storage case.

"Of course," I said with a stiff smile. "Good luck."

"Hey," he said, "what's wrong?"

I stood there, tongue-tied, unable to get my mouth to work.

"I can tell something's bothering you. What is it?"

He looked so earnest and innocent, I was beginning to feel foolish for ever having suspected him. But I had to be sure.

Summoning my courage, I took the plunge.

"I'm embarrassed to ask, but where were you the night of the murder?"

"Wow," he said, wide-eyed. "I'm on your suspect list after all. Do you actually think I killed Bebe?"

"Not really," I admitted. "But I have to ask. Just to ease my mind."

"Consider your mind eased. I was with Mrs. Fletcher, my violin teacher, prepping for the recital. Honest!"

Then he took me by the hand and led me inside to the school auditorium, abuzz with parents clutching video-cams and cell phones.

A plump sixtysomething gal with steel-gray hair crimped into a tortured perm was standing in the aisle, passing out programs. As she greeted her guests, I couldn't help but notice a most unsettling mole on the side of her nose.

"Justin!" she cried, catching sight of him. "Guess what? I invited the music critic from the *Los Angeles Times*, and he said he might be able to make it."

"That's great, Mrs. Fletcher."

"Get ready to be discovered!" she crowed. "And who might this be?" she added, noticing me.

"Mrs. Fletcher, I'd like you to meet my friend Jaine."

"A pleasure, my dear," she said, handing me a program. "Welcome to the annual recital of the Fletcher Music Academy! Are you by any chance interested in taking violin lessons?"

"No, I'm afraid not."

"What a shame! You really ought to consider it. Those long, tapering fingers of yours were made for the violin!"

She sure knew how to sling the bull poo. My fingers, while perfectly serviceable, are far from long and tapering.

"Mrs. Fletcher," Justin broke in, "would you mind

telling Jaine where I was the night Bebe Braddock got killed?"

"With me, like you always are every Monday and Thursday night, taking a violin lesson." She beamed with pride. "Don't tell the others," she whispered conspiratorially, "but Justin is my star pupil!"

"Now am I in the clear?" Justin asked me as we headed down the aisle.

"Absolutely," I nodded, thrilled he had an alibi.

My mind finally at ease, I took a seat while Justin headed backstage to await his time slot.

Meanwhile, as Mrs. Fletcher fluttered about, handing out programs, I heard her whisper to a couple in the row in front of me, "Don't tell the others, but Louisa is my star pupil!"

Why did I get the feeling that all Mrs. Fletcher's pupils were her stars?

Eventually everyone was seated, and Mrs. Fletcher got onstage to thank them for showing up, blabbity blah-ing about how gratifying it had been to work with her students, to see their latent talents blossom before her very eyes.

Then, one by one, her protégées took the stage to do their thing.

Now I'm no music critic, not even close, but I think it's fair to say they were all on the higher end of the stink-o-meter. None of them was about to be discovered by the *Los Angeles Times* or any other reputable news outlet.

Some of them got through their pieces without stumbling too badly, others with more than an occasional wrong note. One kid managed to drop his bow no fewer than three times.

Most of the performers were kids, way younger than Justin.

Each one wrapped up their piece—no matter how faltering—to thunderous applause from family and friends.

Finally it was Justin's turn.

Unlike the other deer-in-the-headlights students, he strode out onto the stage with authority and confidence. Then, tucking his violin under his chin, he began to play.

Surely, he had to be better than the kidlets.

But, alas, he was not. In fact, to be perfectly honest, he was a tad worse. At one point, he hit a screech of a note that sounded a lot like Prozac at the vet's office.

I certainly hoped he had a Plan B career in the works.

He finished to frantic applause from Mrs. Fletcher, took a bow, and looked over at me.

I gave him a thumbs up, a fake smile plastered on my face.

Not a moment too soon, the recital was over, Mrs. Fletcher again thanking everyone for showing up, and blathering on about a discount package she was offering—ten violin lessons for the price of five.

Eventually Justin came out from backstage to join me.

"So? How was I?"

"Great!" I managed to lie, my smile still welded to my face, hoping he was buying it.

"You're not just saying that?"

"No way," I lied again.

"I think I may have missed a note or two."

"If you did, I didn't notice."

One more lie, and I'd be running for Congress.

Just then we were joined by Mrs. Fletcher.

"Bravo!" she gushed. "Wonderful performance, my dear. Absolutely inspiring!"

What the what?!

"Just keep up your lessons for a few more years, and one day you'll be playing that violin at Carnegie Hall!"

Was she kidding? There was no way in hell Justin was ever going to make it as a concert violinist. Clearly Mrs. Fletcher was giving him false encouragement so he'd keep paying for music lessons. What a moneygrubbing old crone.

I was sorely tempted to report her to the Better Business Bureau.

"Isn't she great?" Justin said as we headed out to the parking lot. "Lots of her former students have made it to the LA Philharmonic. I just know I'm going to get there, too."

Somebody needed to tell Justin the truth. But it wasn't going to be me.

Sooner or later, he'd realize he wasn't cut out for the concert stage. With his looks and charm, he'd have lots of doors open to him, for sure. Maybe not the door to Carnegie Hall, but something told me he'd wind up on his feet.

Back at my duplex, he walked me up the front path to my apartment.

A blinding flash of his dimple, and then he zeroed in for a blockbuster kiss.

My lady parts, so recently on life support, were now alive and well and doing the conga.

"I guess I'd better be going," he said, when we finally came up for air. "I don't want to rush into things. That never works in the long run."

For someone so much younger than me, he was awfully wise. I'd been ready to throw caution (and my undies) to the wind.

"And I want this to work," he said, tracing his finger along my cheek.

"Me too," I gulped, my knees now the consistency of Silly Putty.

After another rocketblaster of a kiss, he turned and headed off down the front path.

Justin may have stunk as a violinist, but when it came to smooching, he was a certified virtuoso.

You've Got Mail

To: Jausten
From: Shoptillyoudrop
Subject: Marvelous News!

Marvelous news, sweetheart! I finally finished *War and Peace*. Not the novel, of course, but the movie! Luckily I was able to rent it at the library. A wonderful picture starring Audrey Hepburn, looking ever so lovely as the heroine, Natasha. I'm still having trouble with all those Russian names, but at least I have a vague idea of the plot.

On the irritating front, Daddy's been gone practically every night, tailing Lydia, on his ridiculous mission to catch her in a tryst with a married man. He can follow her all he wants, but he'll never find anything incriminating.

Actually, it's quite peaceful here, without Daddy shouting out the wrong answers to *Jeopardy!* Quite peaceful, indeed.

I bought the wine for the book club today. Think I'll go open a bottle and have a weensy sample.

XOXO,
Mom

To: Jausten
From: DaddyO
Subject: Paydirt!

At last, Lambchop! Tonight I hit paydirt in my search to get the goods on Stinky Pinkus!

She got in her car at about six o'clock, all dolled up and ready for action in what I can only guess was her new Victoria's Secret push-up bra and lace garter belt.

I followed her as she drove out of Tampa Vistas, keeping a careful three car lengths behind. Everything was going smoothly until I got stopped at a red light and watched her speed away. I drove around for a while, certain I'd lost her. Then, just as I was about to throw in the towel and head back home, I spotted her heading into a cozy little restaurant, appropriately called The Hideaway.

I pulled into the parking lot and, after waiting a few minutes, got out of my car and went inside.

The restaurant was a hideaway, all right—dimly lit and lined with red leather booths, Frank Sinatra crooning in the background. The booths were filled with couples holding hands and playing footsies. I couldn't help but notice several older gents taking their "nieces" out to dinner.

It wasn't easy to see in all that gloom, but I soon spotted Lydia in a corner booth, cozying up to a balding guy in a too-tight suit. The man had all the sex appeal of a wet flounder. What a perfect match.

In the glow of the candle flickering at their table, I saw a wedding ring on The Flounder's finger. Bingo! Just the ammunition I was looking for.

I whipped out my cell phone and got a picture of the happy couple—to prove to Mom once and for all that Lydia was having an affair with a married man.

Just as I snapped the photo, I was approached by a goon of a maître d', a hulking brute who looked like he'd tossed more than his fair share of dead bodies in the Hudson River.

"What do you think you're doing, buddy?" he growled.

For the first time, I realized I probably looked out of place in my baseball cap and aviator sunglasses.

"I was just getting a picture of your restaurant to show my wife," I said, in a burst of inspired fibbing. "I want to take her here for our anniversary."

"Yeah, right," said the goon, lobbing me a skeptical look as he shoved me out the door.

But I didn't care. I'd accomplished my mission. I couldn't wait to show your mom the picture of Lydia and her lover.

Unfortunately, when I got back in my car to check my phone, I realized that in my haste to get the shot, my thumb had blocked out Lydia's half of the picture.
But I know what I saw—the revolting sight of The Battle-Axe cozying up to The Flounder!

And I'm more determined than ever to bring her down, toppling her reign of terror at Tampa Vistas!

Love 'n snuggles
From your triumphant,
Daddy

To: Jausten
From: Shoptillyoudrop
Subject: Utter Bilge!

I was nestled down on the sofa just now, watching a relaxing episode of *House Hunters*, when Daddy came barging in the front door, making a ruckus, claiming he had "proof positive" that Lydia is having an affair!

He says he followed her to a restaurant called The Hideaway and swears he saw her in a corner booth with her married lover.

His "proof positive"? A picture of the so-called lovers, with Daddy's thumb blocking out the woman in the picture. What's more, he admits that he lost track of Lydia's car on the ride over to the restaurant, but insists he recognized her heading inside.

Of all the utter bilge! Not only has Daddy needed new glasses for ages, he's notoriously bad at recognizing people. Why, just the other week, he claimed he saw Meryl Streep thumping cantaloupes at the market!

I'm so darn annoyed I never got to see which house Darryl and Kristin of Dallas chose. It was a toss-up between a Craftsman and a ranch, and I was rooting for the Craftsman.

Oh, well. Time for another sip of my book club wine, which is really quite refreshing. Must remember to buy a replacement bottle tomorrow.

XOXO,
Mom

To: Jausten
From: DaddyO
Subject: Advanced Surveillance

Guess what, Lambchop? In my valiant effort to unmask
Stinky Pinkus as the sanctimonious hypocrite she is, I've
decided to go high tech and have just sent away for a drone.
You know, one of those flying metal doohickeys that let you
take video footage from the sky. With this kind of advanced
surveillance, I'm sure to gather all the evidence I need to
convict Stinky in the court of public opinion.

The drone is fairly high tech, but I'm sure I'll get the hang of
it in no time. Stay tuned for further developments from
Tampa Vistas's champion of justice—

—Your ever loving,
Daddy

Chapter 18

The next morning, after treating myself to a delicious cinnamon raisin bagel—and even more delicious daydreams of my smoochfest with Justin—I made the mistake of opening my emails.

I cringed at the thought of Daddy's trip to The Hideaway restaurant, decked out in his baseball cap and 99-cent store sunglasses.

Mom was right, of course. No way was Lydia Pinkus, Tampa Vistas' bastion of respectability, having an affair. Whoever Daddy had seen at The Hideaway, it sure as heck hadn't been Lydia.

Eager to escape the drama at Tampa Vistas, I closed out my emails and turned my attention back where it belonged—to Bebe's murder.

I definitely needed to have a chat with Anna, the adulterous seamstress, so I texted her, asking if I could drop by.

"K" she texted back.

Not exactly brimming with hospitality, but at least she hadn't turned me down.

It was a tough slog through L.A.'s always torturous traffic, but eventually I made it to Anna's place in Hollywood—a weary looking box of a building that had probably looked shabby back when it was brand new.

Now it was far from new, painted a muddy brown, lined with settling cracks, and dotted with water stains. A sign out front informed me that I'd arrived at Sunset Gardens.

Whatever gardens had once been there were long gone. The only greenery I saw were the weeds coming up through the cracks in the sidewalk.

The security gate was unlatched, so I let myself into a tiny courtyard with a postage stamp-sized pool. Floating on the pool's murky surface were a Frisbee and several cans of Bud Light. A snoring slacker was sprawled out on a deck chair—the source, I suspected, of the floating beer cans.

Scooting past him, I climbed a metal staircase to Anna's second-floor apartment and rang the bell. Seconds later, the door was opened by a cute young thing in cutoffs and a tank top.

I was just about to ask where Anna was when I realized the cute young thing *was* Anna. What a far cry from the timid critter in the seamstress smock kneeling at my knees, her mouth full of pins.

Up close, I could see a definite resemblance to Bebe. But while everything seemed pinched on Bebe, Anna's features were gentler—her lips just a bit fuller, her eyes a bit wider. Looking at her was like looking at Bebe through a soft-focus lens.

"C'mon in," she said, ushering me into a cramped living room, furnished with what looked like a combination of thrift shop finds and castoffs from Bebe.

The only window in the room provided a depressing view of the neighboring apartment building.

"If I'm not careful," she said, following my gaze, "I can see Mr. Boyarsky across the way showering. And trust me, that's not a pretty picture.

"Have a seat," she said.

I plopped down on her sofa as she snapped on a pair of rubber gloves.

"I hope you don't mind if I do some cleaning while we talk. I need to stay busy to get my mind off Bebe."

What exactly was she so eager to get her mind off? I wondered. Feelings of grief—or guilt?

"No problem," I said.

With that, she began dusting an étagère jammed with knickknacks and photos. I couldn't help but notice that her dust rag was a TEAM BEBE T-shirt.

So much for team spirit.

"I'm so sorry about Bebe," I said. "My sincere condolences for having to put up with such a dreadful sister for all those years."

Okay, so I didn't say the last part, but I was thinking it.

"I still can't believe she's gone," Anna sighed.

Then she picked up a framed photo from the étagère and brought it over to me.

"Here's a picture of me and Bebe with our parents when we first came to the United States."

I looked down at a faded photo of Anna's family. Her parents stood stiffly in heavy overcoats, unwilling or unable to smile for the camera, two little towheaded girls at their side.

"We came here with only the clothes on our back, and all the family valuables sewn into the lining of Mama's coat. That's me," she said, pointing to the younger of the two girls, clinging to her mother. "I was a scared little kid. Not like Bebe. Look at her."

She pointed to the older girl, standing straight, chin up, a determined smile on her face.

"Bebe was the brave one in the family. She picked up English right away, made lots of friends. She was even a cheerleader in high school. Then after graduation, she sold one of Mama's brooches, got herself a good haircut and nice clothes, and landed a job at Macy's. That's where Tatiana discovered her and hired her as her assistant. Before long, Bebe was doing so well, she left Tatiana to start her own business.

"And every step of the way," she said, putting the photo back on the étagère, "she always took care of me."

This is how she took care of you? I looked around the shabby room with the view of Mr. Boyarsky's bathroom. *Paying slave wages and treating you like dirt?*

As if reading my thoughts, Anna said, "I know Bebe could be rough on me, but underneath it all, she was a loving sister, and I'm going to miss her terribly."

This little tribute might have been very moving had I not known about Anna's affair with Miles. And it was hard (actually, impossible) to picture Bebe loving anyone but herself. I felt certain Anna would survive quite nicely without her.

"I suppose you know I'm a suspect in the case," I said, getting down to business.

"Yes, I heard they found your fingerprints on the murder weapon."

Thank you, Motormouth Miles.

"I swear, I didn't kill your sister."

"If you say so," she said with a shrug. "Sorry, no disrespect, but it's hard to know who or what to believe."

My sentiments exactly.

"Do you have any idea who might have killed Bebe?" I asked. "Aside from me?"

"If I had to guess, I'd say Tatiana. She never really forgave Bebe for walking away with so many of her clients. I think she's been nursing a powerful grudge all these years."

True. But remembering how miserably Bebe had treated Anna, I wondered if Anna hadn't been nursing a powerful grudge of her own.

"Well, that's done," Anna said, wiping the last of the dust from the étagère.

She pulled off her rubber gloves, and for the first time I noticed something very interesting—a bandage on the palm of her right hand.

"What happened to your hand?" I asked.

"Oh, that," she said, jerking her hand behind her back. "I cut myself with a seam ripper."

Was it my imagination or did she seem distinctly uncomfortable?

Maybe she'd cut her hand with a seam ripper. Or maybe, just maybe, she cut it with the sharp edge of a wire hanger as she twisted it into a noose.

Chapter 19

Back in my Corolla, I checked my cell phone and found a text from the *L.A. Times* reminding me of my interview with Prozac at eleven that morning.

Yikes. I'd forgotten all about it.

I'd just have time to race home and gussy myself up for the camera. I was determined to look as good as possible and counteract that ghastly image of my tush currently circulating in cyberspace.

Just my luck, I ran into a traffic jam in the heart of Beverly Hills (where traffic jams tend to look like a Mercedes Benz parking lot), and by the time I got home, I had little more than a half hour to prep.

As I dashed up the front path, Lance came ambling out of his apartment, tanned and buff, in his gym togs.

"Hey, Jaine," he said. "How's it going?"

"No time to talk, Lance. The reporter from the *L.A. Times* will be here soon, and I've got to hurry."

"What reporter from the *L.A. Times*?"

"Didn't I tell you? They want to do an interview about Prozac saving that toddler's life."

"No, you didn't tell me. How exciting! Let me know how it goes."

And off he trotted to perfect his already perfect body at the gym.

Racing into my apartment, I found Prozac hard at work on one of her power naps. I hurried past her to my bedroom, where I scoured my closet for an interview outfit. Working on the assumption that the camera would add ten unwanted pounds, I decided on a black cashmere crewneck and indigo skinny jeans.

Next it was time to do my makeup. Usually I just slap on some lipstick and go, but today I went the whole nine yards—foundation, blush, and mascara. I even managed a quickie eyebrow tweeze.

Prozac, who had roused herself from her slumber and was now perched on the toilet tank, watched me do my makeup with a distinct air of superiority.

Lucky for me, I'm a natural beauty. So I never have to primp and fuss.

I polished off my beauty regimen by scrunching my hair with some curl-defining gel and surveyed myself in the bathroom mirror.

Not bad. Not bad at all.

If I played my cards right, soon the new improved version of me would be obliterating my ghastly cyber tush.

A quick spritz of cologne and I was ready for my close-up. And not a moment too soon. Because just then the reporter showed up.

She turned out to be a young gal in her early twenties. Very early twenties.

"Hi," she introduced herself, "I'm Sarita Mehta from the *Los Angeles Times*."

"So nice to meet you." I looked around for a photographer, but Sarita appeared to be all alone.

No photographer? Phooey! Don't tell me I'd done all that primping for nothing?!

"Isn't somebody going to be taking pictures for this story?" I asked, ushering her inside.

"Yes, me. I'll be reporting—and taking pictures, too. The *Times* usually saves full-time photographers for breaking news stories."

Well, that was a relief. The new improved me would be in the paper after all.

"Have a seat," I said, gesturing to my overstuffed chintz armchair.

"I hope you don't mind if I record our session," she said, taking a slim silver mini-recorder from her purse and placing it on the coffee table.

"Not at all."

"So where's this heroic cat of yours?" she asked, looking around.

Last time I saw her, my heroic cat had been clawing my toilet paper to ribbons.

"Prozac, honey!" I called out. "Come here and meet the nice reporter from the newspaper!"

Normally, Prozac ignores any and all requests I make, but I swear that cat understands English. She knew something important was afoot, because seconds later, she came prancing into the living room, swishing her tail proudly.

Here I am! The Cat Who Saved a Toddler's Life!

She looked up at Sarita and stopped in her tracks, clearly unimpressed.

Wait, what? You're not famous. Where's Anderson Cooper? Shouldn't he be covering this story?

"C'mon, Pro," I said, scooping her up in my arms. "Sit on Mommy's lap while she chats with the nice lady."

She instantly wriggled free from my grasp.

I don't feel like sitting on your lap. And how many times have I told you? You're not my mommy!

With that, she leaped onto the coffee table, riveted by the sight of Sarita's recorder.

What's this? A present for moi to destroy?

Before I could stop her, she'd swiped it off the table with her paw, her killer instinct ignited.

Prepare to meet your death, shiny silver thing!

Luckily I managed to grab her just as she was about to pounce on the recorder.

"I'm so sorry," I said to Sarita.

"That's okay," she replied with a weak smile. "I guess I'd better keep it in my lap."

I could almost hear her thinking, *For this I spent two years at Columbia Journalism school?*

"So," she said, her hand hovering protectively over the recorder, "tell me all about how Prozac saved that toddler's life."

Oh, how I wanted to tell her the truth, that my feline foodie was only in it for the chicken nugget. But I couldn't risk missing out on a flattering picture in the paper.

So I dove right in and told tell her the fairy tale version of the story, with Prozac selflessly racing in the path of an oncoming car to push Trevor out of harm's way.

"That's really remarkable," Sarita said.

Prozac preened.

Not only that, I vanquished the evil alien from the Planet Acorn. Not to mention some extremely dangerous pantyhose and several pot holders possessed by the devil!

"So tell me all about your relationship with Prozac," Sarita said. "How long have you had her? What are her favorite foods? Why did you name her Prozac?"

You'd think by now the answer to that last one would have been obvious, but I was more than happy to oblige her with some chatter.

"Well," I said, but before I could get to Syllable Two, there was a knock on my front door.

"Yoo hoo, Jaine! It's me, Lance!"

Oh, jeez. The egomaniac had come to horn in on my interview.

With a sigh, I got up and opened the door to find him all spiffed up in jeans and a tight-fitting tee. He obviously never went to the gym; instead he sneaked back to his apartment to prep for the interview.

"I hope I'm not intruding," he said, barging right in, "but when Jaine told me she was doing an interview with the *L.A. Times,* I knew I had to stop by. Prozac and I are incredibly close. I'm her godfather, you know."

Really? That was news to me.

"Allow me to introduce myself. I'm Jaine's beloved neighbor, Lance Venable, V-E-N-A-B-L-E.

"Prozac, honeybunch," he cooed, spotting her. "How's my rescuing angel?"

Pro, the little traitor, purred at the sight of him, and leaped into his lap as he joined me on the sofa. Which was most galling, considering she'd been wriggling out of my grasp from the start of the interview.

"She really seems to like you," Sarita said to Lance, as Prozac practically swooned in his arms.

"She does indeed. I guess you could say I'm her role model. Cats are very observant creatures," he said, suddenly anointing himself a zoologist. "Prozac gets her fondness of food from Jaine, and her charitable instincts from me. I'm a longtime supporter of organizations that deliver food to the hungry."

Yeah, right. If by "organizations that deliver food to the hungry" he meant Grubhub and DoorDash.

"And Prozac's bravery in times of crisis?" Lance blathered on. "She gets that from me, too. Why, just last year, I rescued my uncle from drowning."

"Really?" Sarita perked up, interested. "How?"

"Well, he'd had a tad too much to drink at Thanksgiving dinner and fell face down into the pumpkin soup. I was the one who grabbed him by his few remaining hairs and yanked him out of the soup tureen."

Wow, somebody get this guy a Purple Heart.

Showing no shame, Lance continued to highjack the interview, horning in on every question Sarita lobbed my way. The way he was nattering on about Prozac, you'd think he'd given birth to her.

As I recall, my total contribution to the rest of the interview was, "I adopted her from a pet shelter."

By this point, I was ready to throttle Lance, but at last Sarita said she was ready to take some pictures.

Lance was all set to pose with Prozac, but Sarita, bless her heart, told Lance she wanted only a picture of me and Prozac together.

Lance reluctantly handed Prozac to me, and needless to say, the minute she was in my lap, she started squirming to break free. I finally managed to get her to sit still with some kitty caviar treats (another gift from Trevor's mom), and Sarita snapped several pictures with her cell phone.

"Thanks so much for your time," she said when she was done, eagerly gathering her things, no doubt wishing she were reporting an actual story.

"A pleasure to meet you!" Lance called after her as she hustled out the door. "Remember that's Venable. V-E-N-A-B-L-E."

The minute Sarita left, I whirled on Lance, furious.

"Lance V-E-N-A-B-L-E, I can't believe you had the nerve to bust in here and hijack my interview!"

"Gosh, hon. I'm sorry. Was I talking too much?"

"Only nonstop, the Niagara Falls of chitchat."

"I was just so excited about Prozac, I guess I got carried away. But you could've jumped in any time."

"Are you kidding? I'd need a jackhammer to get a word in edgewise."

"My bad," he said, abashed. "I didn't mean to steal your thunder." He held out his arms for a hug. "Forgive me?"

In spite of myself, I could feel my anger melting. He looked as sorry as a puppy who'd just pooped on the carpet. And besides, all I really cared about was getting my picture in the paper.

"You're forgiven," I said sliding into his arms.

"By the way," he said when we broke apart, "I haven't forgotten about helping you solve Bebe's murder. I'm more certain than ever that Sven Gustafson is the killer."

Lance sure seemed eager to pin the murder on his handsome blond coworker.

"He's been acting really strange at Neiman's lately, very antsy and nervous, and when I brought up the subject of Bebe's death, he just muttered something under his breath and hurried off to the stock room."

"Here's a wild idea: Maybe he went to get a pair of shoes."

"No, he's the killer, all right. There's only one tiny fly in the ointment."

"Which is?"

"He claims he was on vacation in Oslo the night of the murder."

"A tiny fly? Sounds more like an airtight alibi to me."

"Not necessarily, my dear Watson. It just so happens Sven has a twin brother, Lars.

"Lars could have easily flown to Oslo using Sven's passport, while Sven stayed here in Los Angeles to kill Bebe. I told you how furious he was when Bebe dumped him as her shoe salesman."

"That doesn't seem like much of a motive for murder to me."

"Trust me, Jaine. I can read people like a book, and this guy has 'guilty' written all over him. I already phoned in an anonymous tip to the police, so they're bound to arrest him any day now."

Why did I get the feeling that Lance's anonymous tip had been filed away in a handy trash can? Not for a minute did I believe Sven faked a trip to Oslo to kill Bebe.

"And I promise when I'm interviewed for solving the murder, I'll let you do all the talking. Now I really must run to the gym," he said, giving me a quick peck on the cheek.

"Bye, sweetpea!" he called out to Prozac before sailing out the door.

I looked over at Prozac, busy examining her genitals.

Now it was her turn in the hot seat.

"And you, you ungrateful wretch," I said, glaring at her, "ignoring me while that reporter was here, wriggling out of my arms like you'd never even met me, like I haven't been keeping you up to your eyeballs in minced mackerel guts and belly rubs all these years."

She looked up from her privates, startled.

"Well, there'll be no belly rubs in your future, young lady. Not from me. Not for a very long time."

I guess she could see how ticked off I was because she instantly abandoned her gynecological exam and came scampering over to me, rubbing herself against my ankles, mewing plaintively, little Ms. Lovable.

"Forget it," I said, walking away with a hardened heart.

She wasn't going to worm her way back into my good graces that easily.

No, siree. No way. I was tough. I was firm. I was the strict disciplinarian she so rightly deserved.

You'll be proud to know I waited a full twelve minutes before swooping her up in my arms for a belly rub.

Purring contentedly, she looked up at me with big green eyes that could mean only one thing:

I'm so sorry I hurt your feelings. Got any more caviar treats?

Chapter 20

"Whatever you're selling, I don't want any!" Tatiana Rogers shrieked before hanging up on me.

I'd called Bebe's tempestuous former boss and rival stylist to set up a visit, but I could see it wasn't going to be easy.

It took three more phone calls before I finally convinced her I wasn't a telemarketer.

"Then who are you?"

"Jaine Austen. We met at Bebe's studio; I was there getting a makeover when you dropped in." Notice how I diplomatically avoided any mention of her blazing meltdown. "Afterward, we had tea and brownies with Miles in the kitchen."

"Right. I remember. Boy, you sure can pack away those brownies."

Now I was the one who wanted to hang up on her. Instead, I forced a weak, "Haha. That's me."

"Miles says your fingerprints were found all over the murder weapon."

"Actually, that's why I'm calling. I'm hoping to clear my name, and I was wondering if I could stop by for a chat."

"Why do you want to talk to me?" she asked warily.

"I'm trying to learn all I can about Bebe, any scrap of information that might lead me to the killer."

Who might very well be you, I refrained from adding.

"I'll be tied up with clients all morning," she said. "You can stop by later this afternoon. I'll text you my address."

I thanked her and hung up, more than a tad ticked off.

Not at her brownie crack (although that was pretty darn annoying). No, the person I wanted to slap silly was Miles Braddock, running around telling practically everyone in Los Angeles County my fingerprints had been found on the murder weapon.

Clearly he was going out of his way to throw me under the bus. Perhaps because he was trying to deflect attention away from the real killer—Miles himself.

Time to pay another visit to the merry widower.

Casa Braddock looked the same as the day I first showed up, the front yard lush with flowers.

But somehow the flowers seemed brighter, more vivid, now that Bebe was gone. Even the birds seemed to be chirping a happier tune.

There was no answer when I rang the bell, so I decided to go around the side of the house to the backyard, just in case Miles was lounging at the pool, checking out vacation destinations for a romantic getaway with Anna.

The pool was deserted when I got there, and I was just about to turn around and go back to my Corolla when I noticed the French doors to Bebe's studio were open.

Maybe Miles was there, gathering Bebe's wooden hangers for a bonfire.

So I wandered over to the studio—only to get the shock of my life when I looked in and saw Miles slumped over Bebe's desk.

Oh, hell. It was déjà vu all over again! Was I about to discover yet another dead body?

I tiptoed closer to Miles, already cringing at the thought of being questioned by Detective Washington.

Then suddenly Miles snorted awake, startled at the sight of me.

"Hi, Miles," I said, flooded with relief. "Sorry I woke you."

"That's okay."

He quickly slammed shut a large, ledger-sized checkbook on the desk in front of him.

But not quickly enough to keep me from seeing a check made out to Beverly Hills Maserati.

Somebody was on a buying spree now that his wife was dead.

"What can I do for you?" he asked, a flicker of impatience in his eyes.

"Actually, I need to talk to you about Bebe's murder."

"What about it?"

"I happened to stop by the El Dorado Cigar Lounge the other night, and your friend Eddie confirmed what you told me. He said you were there until ten PM the night of the murder."

"Sounds like you were checking up on me."

"Kinda sorta," I admitted.

"Do you really think I killed Bebe?"

"Anything's possible."

Not the answer he wanted to hear.

"If Eddie told you I was there all night," he said, shooting me a death ray glare, "why are you here? What else do you need to know?"

Okay, time for me to unleash the lie I'd dreamed up on the drive over.

"Eddie may not have seen you leave the lounge, but I

was talking to another patron who was there that night, and he told me he saw you walking out the door well before ten o'clock."

Yes, this was a whopper of the highest order. As you well know (if you were paying attention and not checking your pockets for stray M&M's), I'd spoken to no such person. But I was a desperado.

And guess what? It worked.

"Okay," he snapped. "So I left the lounge. I went to visit Bebe's sister, Anna."

"Really?" I asked, all wide-eyed, as if I hadn't seen them smooching at Bebe's funeral.

"Yes, we've grown quite close over the years."

I'll say, I thought, remembering how they were practically welded together in the chapel hallway.

"I trust you won't be telling anyone about this," he said, getting up from the desk and walking over to me. "For your sake, as well as mine."

Gulp. He was a lot taller than I remembered. And bulkier, too. Up to then, Miles had seemed like a lumbering teddy bear of a guy. But that teddy bear had just morphed into a grizzly.

I was beginning to feel a wee bit terrified.

"We wouldn't want anything to happen to those pretty curls of yours, would we?" Now he was at my side, running the tips of his fingers along my hair.

"Nope, we definitely don't want that," I stammered.

And with that, I raced out of the studio and back to my Corolla as fast as my trembling legs could carry me.

I knew a threat when I heard one, and I'd darn well just heard one.

With every beat of my wildly thumping heart, I grew more convinced that Miles was the killer. I could almost see his beefy hands tightening the noose around Bebe's neck.

But I couldn't rule out Tatiana. Not yet, anyway.

After a pit stop at Mickey D's for a calming Quarter Pounder, I headed out to the San Fernando Valley to Tatiana's rustic bungalow in Canoga Park.

And by "rustic" I mean *thisclose* to being condemned.

With peeling paint, rotting shingles, and settling cracks the size of the San Andreas fault, it looked like the only thing keeping the place together were termites holding hands.

I knocked on the front door, hoping it wouldn't fall off its hinges.

Inside I could hear the sound of shuffling footsteps, and soon the door swung open, revealing Tatiana in a stained kimono, gray roots sprouting in her jet-black hair.

In her hand, she held a filled-to-the-brim margarita glass.

"Jaine, dear. How nice to see you again!"

From the potent blast of tequila on her breath, I was guessing one of the "clients" she'd been entertaining earlier that day was Jose Cuervo.

"Come on in!" she said, beaming me a smile, so much friendlier than she'd been on the phone that morning. Maybe she thought I'd actually killed Bebe and was bubbling over with gratitude.

I stepped into her living room, a tiny box of a space crammed with once-expensive silk-upholstered furniture, now dotted with stains and worn thin at the armrests.

Taking up an entire wall was a clothes rack, whose garments, I couldn't help but notice, were all hanging on wire hangers.

"Welcome to my L.A. studio," she said with a flourish, the contents of her margarita sloshing over the rim of the glass. "It's my pied-à-terre when I'm here in town. My other home is in Montecito."

Oh, please. Did she honestly expect me to believe she had a place in Montecito, a city so expensive you needed a cosigner to check out at the local market?

"Care for a margarita?"

She nodded in the direction of her kitchen, where I saw a blender full of the stuff.

"I'm fine," I said, perching my fanny on her fraying sofa.

"Guess what I found in my samples!" She flitted over to the clothing rack. "A fabulous Michael Kors cocktail dress."

She held out a leopard-print number with a plunging neckline and a peplum at the waist.

"Isn't it perfect?"

Only if you were a hooker soliciting johns on Sunset Boulevard.

"Very nice," I said with a weak smile, pretty sure I'd seen something very much like it on clearance at T. J. Maxx.

"I thought of you the minute I saw it," Tatiana cooed. "It's only been worn once, and I'm prepared to let it go for just five thousand dollars!"

Was she kidding? If I had five grand to spare, I'd have hired myself a defense attorney instead of running around town trying to clear my name.

"Sorry, but that's way too expensive for me."

"How about two thousand?" she asked with a desperate smile. "One thou? . . . Okay, five hundred, and it's yours."

"Honestly, Tatiana. I don't have that kind of money."

And with that, her smile vanished, along with much of her margarita.

"Okay," she said, sprawling out across from me on the sofa, her kimono opening perilously close to her G-spot. "What do you want to know?"

"Like I said on the phone, I'm looking for any info you can give me about Bebe, her friends, her life, her background."

"Friends?" She laughed bitterly. "Bebe had no friends. The woman was toxic. And all I know about Bebe's background is that story she was constantly telling about her parents showing up in this country with only the clothes on their back and their valuables hidden in her mom's coat. Frankly, I wouldn't be surprised if she made the whole thing up to add some spice to her bio. For all I know, she was born in Topeka and was president of her 4-H club."

She paused in her tirade to guzzle down the rest of her margarita.

"Bebe could be a real charmer when she wanted. She sure had me snowed. I thought I'd found the perfect assistant, until she upped and walked away with half my client list."

She shook her head, still stung by the memory.

"After all I did for her, all the gifts I lavished on her. Hermès scarves. Burberry coats. And that fabulous Birkin handbag!"

I remembered the red leather purse I'd seen in Bebe's studio.

"That thing's gotta be worth a fortune today."

"It must have been quite a blow when she left you," I said, in my best empathetic therapist voice. "I could see how angry you were that day you showed up to confront her. I remember your saying something about how someday Bebe would get what she deserved."

With that, Tatiana snapped out of her margarita haze, her eyes suddenly narrowed and alert.

"If you think I had anything to do with Bebe's murder, think again, honey. I was home all night, watching *Project Runway* reruns."

"Gosh, no," I lied. "I didn't suspect you at all."

"When I made that crack about Bebe getting what she deserved, I only meant I wanted to see her business go up in flames. I was furious with her for stealing Lacey Hunt out from under me. But kill her? Never! If I killed everyone who's screwed me in this town, I would've been behind bars years ago.

"In fact, if you ask me, the killer might well be Lacey."

"Lacey Hunt?" It was hard to picture the freckled-face young actress as a killer.

"Yes, Lacey. She felt terrible about leaving me. I could tell she didn't really want to work with Bebe. You know what I think?" she said, licking the remaining shards of salt from her margarita glass. "I think Bebe was holding something over Lacey's head, something damaging, and she was blackmailing her into becoming her client."

Could Tatiana possibly be right? Was the budding young movie star Bebe's killer? A very interesting theory, and one I definitely intended to pursue.

"I hate to rush you, sweetie," Tatiana said, eyeing her now empty glass, "but I've got another client coming soon."

"Right. Sure. I understand."

She wasted no time hustling me out the door, and the last thing I heard as I headed down the front path was the faint whir of the blender.

Make way for Señor Cuervo.

*　*　*

It was after five when I left Tatiana, and I was dreading the thought of inching my way home in rush hour traffic. But then I remembered Felipe's niece, Gloria, the lucky recipient of my Cuckoo for Cocoa Puffs T-shirt.

Felipe had written down her address on a slip of paper that I'd shoved in my purse. I vaguely recalled it was somewhere out in the Valley. So I rooted around my tote and finally found it, stuck to a half-eaten Almond Joy.

It turned out Gloria lived in Reseda, just a short hop from Canoga Park, and after Google-mapping the directions, I set out to retrieve my treasured tee.

Soon I was pulling up in front of Gloria's house—a modest bungalow a lot like Tatiana's. Only hers had a fresh coat of paint and a well-tended front yard.

A Tinkerbell sprite answered the door, clad in bike shorts and sports bra. Not an ounce of fat anywhere.

I'd eaten pizzas heavier than her.

"Oh, hi," she said with a bright smile. "Are you here about the room for rent?"

"No, afraid not."

"Darn! People have been canceling out on me all day. If I don't find a new roommate soon to help with the rent, I'm going to get evicted for sure."

"So sorry about that," I said, looking past her into her living room, an airy space furnished from the Ikea Dorm Room collection.

"How can I help you?" she asked.

"I'm Jaine Austen. Your Uncle Felipe told me he gave you my Cuckoo for Cocoa Puffs T-shirt."

"Jane Austen? That name sounds awfully familiar."

"You're probably thinking of the author."

"What author?"

Obviously not an English major.

"She wrote *Pride and Prejudice. Emma. Mansfield Park.*"

"Was she just on *Good Morning America*, promoting her new book?"

"I doubt it. She's been dead three hundred years."

"Oh, well. The name still sounds familiar. I'm sure I've heard it somewhere before."

Time to stop this stroll down literary memory lane.

"As I was saying, your uncle told me he gave you my CUCKOO FOR COCOA PUFFS T-shirt."

"I love that tee!" she grinned. "It's so cool. I've been wearing it as a sleep shirt."

She was wearing my tee as a sleep shirt? The same tee that was a teensy bit tight around my hips?

Why did I suddenly feel like the Incredible Hulk?

"Come on in." Gloria beckoned me inside. "I was just lifting weights."

I followed her into her living room, where she picked up a pair of weights from her coffee table and began hoisting them over her head, her fat-free arms pumping like pistons.

"Weights are great for body sculpting. Do you ever use them?"

"All the time."

Which was technically true, if by "weights" you mean pints of Chunky Monkey.

"Anyhow, I was wondering if I could have my T-shirt back. It's got a lot of sentimental value."

"I'd love to give it to you," she said, arms still churning up and down, "but I can't. Cindy stole it."

"Cindy?"

"My ex-roommate. She nabbed it when she moved out. Along with my juicer and my yoga mat."

Damn that Bebe for ripping it off my body in the first place. I sincerely hoped she was being forced to wear polyester pantsuits in hell.

"Can you give me Cindy's new address?"

"I wish. If I knew where she lived, I could get my stuff back."

"So you have no idea where I can find her?"

"You could try the Sugar Shack. A dive bar down in Redondo Beach. Cindy used to Jello-wrestle there every other Sunday. Maybe you could catch her there."

"Okay, thanks," I said. "Now I'd better get home and feed my cat. If I'm late with her dinner, there's hell to pay."

"Your cat? Now I know why the name Jaine Austen sounds so familiar. I just read about you online. Your cat saved a toddler's life!"

With that, she put down her weights and grabbed her iPad from the coffee table, then tapped the screen until she found what she was looking for.

"Here it is! From the *Los Angeles Times*."

Omigosh. Sarita's article was out!

I snatched the tablet from Gloria, eager to check out my photo, confident that my tush would be nowhere in sight.

I scrolled down past the blather about Pro until I finally came to the picture.

Oh, groan. Double groan.

True, there was no sign of my tush, but Sarita had zoomed in on Prozac, cropping practically all of me out of the picture—all of me, except for my thighs, which looked like two redwoods stranded on a sofa cushion.

First my tush. Now my thighs! What was next? My tummy? My muffin top? Spinach on my teeth?

"Your cat's adorable," Gloria was saying, breaking into my mental hissy fit.

And it was true. Prozac, the little devil, a cat who couldn't have cared less about saving a toddler's life, looked terrific.

While I, a woman who selflessly and almost single-handedly has kept Ben & Jerry's in business for years, got nothing but unflattering body parts in cyberspace.

I thanked Gloria for her time and stomped back to my Corolla, cursing the injustice of it all.

But then, sitting in my car, I had an epiphany. Maybe my body parts orbiting in cyberspace was the universe's way of telling me it was time to drop a few pounds.

Maybe this was a good thing, after all.

And so I vowed then and there to go on a diet.

Which I'd start the minute I finished that half-eaten Almond Joy.

Chapter 21

I was slathering strawberry jam on my cinnamon raisin bagel the next morning, my new diet having lasted all of twelve hours (eight of which I'd spent sleeping).

I guess I was absent the day they handed out willpower. But I didn't feel too guilty.

I read somewhere that dieting isn't good for you, that gaining and losing weight causes all sorts of problems. So I was actually doing the healthy thing, I told myself, as I slathered another glob of jam on my bagel.

Settling down on my sofa with my bagel and a cup of coffee, I eyed the *Los Angeles Times* on my coffee table, still in its plastic wrapper.

If I'd been smart, I would've tossed it straight into the trash, but like a fool, I opened it and cringed to see my mega-thighs splashed all over the front of the Metro section.

If anything, they looked even bigger than they had yesterday. Heck, if they were any bigger, they'd need their own special section.

Disgusted, I tossed the paper on the floor.

Prozac, who has an uncanny ability to sense anything to do with herself, jumped down from where she'd been draped on my armchair and pranced over to look at it.

Her tail thumped in approval.

My, one of us is certainly photogenic, aren't I?

I was seriously considering writing an angry Letter to the Editor with a blistering critique of their photo-cropping techniques when my phone rang.

It was Lance.

"Exciting news, hon! I've got proof positive that Sven is the killer!"

"What proof?"

"I can't talk now. Meet me for lunch, one o'clock at Neiman's café, and I will reveal all."

"Do we have to eat at Neiman's? Can't we go someplace where the prices are in the single digits?"

"No," he decreed. "And by the way, I saw the story about Prozac in the paper today."

"Well? What did you think?"

"I ordered you a Thighmaster."

"Thanks tons," I snarled.

"No need to thank me, honey. You can pay me back later."

And before I could object, he'd hung up.

How aggravating. The last thing I needed was a stupid Thighmaster. I already had two others he'd given me stashed in my hall closet.

So I did what I often do in times of stress.

I took several deep breaths, sent out positive thoughts to the universe, and nuked myself another bagel.

The café at Neiman Marcus was crowded with Botoxed fashionistas, shoving food around their plates, careful to keep their forks from making contact with their lips.

Lance sat across from me, bursting to tell me his news, but I made him wait while I surveyed the menu, a spartan affair consisting mainly of salads and veggie bowls. The most edible thing I could find was a tuna melt.

"What does it come with?" I asked our actor-waiter when he came to take our order.

"Just the plate," he smirked before sprinting off to the kitchen.

I certainly hoped he wasn't expecting a big tip.

"Okay, so what's up?" I asked Lance when we were alone. "Where's your proof that Sven is the killer?"

"Right in here!"

With that, he took a hanky from his pocket and reached into a Neiman Marcus shopping bag.

"Ta da!" he exclaimed, pulling out a paper coffee cup, holding it gingerly with his hanky.

"A coffee cup? That's it?"

"Not just any coffee cup. Sven's coffee cup. I followed him into the break room this morning and fished it out of the trash after he tossed it there."

"So the guy drinks coffee. How does that prove he killed Bebe?"

"His DNA, silly. It's all over the cup. I'm going to take it to the police and have them match it up with DNA found at the crime scene. And voilà! Case solved! I'll be hailed as a civic hero!"

I was having a hard time believing Lance would be hailed as anything other than a nutcase since, last I heard, Sven was in Oslo the night of the murder. Not for a minute did I believe Lance's cockamamie Twin Accomplice theory.

Our chow showed up then, just in the nick of time, giving me something to do while Lance blathered on about his life as a civic hero.

He was in the middle of a mind-numbing debate with himself, deciding what to wear for his first TV interview (a toss-up between Armani and Hugo Boss) when suddenly he froze.

"Omigosh," he cried. "There he is!"

"Who? Armani? Hugo Boss?"

"No, Sven."

I turned to see the same handsome blond guy I'd seen at Bebe's funeral. He stood in the café entrance, glowering, his eyes scanning the room.

Then he spotted Lance and came storming over to our table.

Gulping in dismay, Lance quickly stashed his Neiman Marcus shopping bag out of sight.

"Hey, bro," Lance said, all smiles, the portrait of a phony in action. "How's it going? I'd like you to meet my dear friend, Jaine Austen. Her cat saved a toddler's life."

But Sven didn't care about me or my toddler-saving cat, glaring at Lance with ice in his Nordic veins.

"What the hell were you doing taking my coffee cup out of the trash?"

"Oh, that!" Lance said, with what was meant to be a jolly laugh but came out more like an asthmatic wheeze. "It's for an art project I'm making—a coffee cup collage! I'm so into collages these days. Last week, I made one of plastic sporks. It's all part of my Paper or Plastic collection."

As with my toddler-saving cat, Sven appeared to have no interest in Lance's artistic endeavors.

"Don't think I haven't noticed you sneaking around, following me."

"Who, me?" Lance cried, his eyes wide with fake innocence. "I haven't been following you."

"Are you kidding? You've been like a piece of toilet paper stuck to my shoe. And I'm damn sick of it."

I could practically feel the rage radiating from his designer suit.

"Stay away from me," he said, pulling Lance out of his seat by his tie, "or I'll be reporting you to Human Resources. And stay away from Marjorie Hoffstatter, too," he added as he shoved Lance back down. "She's my client, and I don't want you poaching her like you did with Bebe Braddock."

Then he turned on his heels and stalked out of the café.

"See?" Lance said. "I told you he was a loose cannon."

I had to admit Sven seemed more than a tad explosive.

Could Lance possibly be right? Was Sven the killer? Had he been furious with Bebe for dumping him, a fury that ballooned into first-degree murder?

Just something to ponder as I picked the potato chunks out of Lance's veggie bowl.

After lunch, Lance went to his locker to stow Sven's purloined DNA, while I took the elevator down to the main level. Over in the shoe department, I saw Sven sliding designer pumps on a perfectly coiffed one-percenter, who beamed in the warmth of his smile.

If I hadn't just seen his roiling fury at the café, I'd never guess he had an angry bone in his body.

I started for the exit, but not without a pit stop at the Jo Malone perfume counter.

I don't know if you've ever tried her stuff, but Jo Malone makes the most heavenly scents this side of the Garden of Eden. My favorite is Nectarine Blossom and Honey, and whenever I'm at Neiman's, I stop by for a free tester spritz.

I was mid-spritz, sniffing the heady aroma of sweet nectarines, when I happened to glance across the aisle at a scarf display. Standing there, admiring the scarves, was a cute young thing wearing a floppy hat and oversized sunglasses. The wide brim of her hat covered much of her face, but at this angle I could see a sprinkling of freckles across her tiny nose.

Something about that freckled face looked familiar.

Just as I was trying to figure out where I'd seen her before, she took the scarf she'd been admiring and—much to my amazement—slipped it in her tote.

Yikes! I'd just witnessed a shoplifter in action!

I looked around to see if anyone else had noticed, but the saleswoman at the scarf counter was oblivious, helping another customer.

Mesmerized, I watched as the freckled-faced shoplifter sauntered over to the costume jewelry counter and nabbed a faux pearl bracelet, sliding it into her tote with the sleight of hand of a trained magician.

As she did, I noticed a fringe of red bangs poking out from under the brim of her hat.

Then it all came together: The freckles. The tiny nose. The red hair.

I remembered where I'd seen them before—in Bebe's studio. If I wasn't mistaken, the cutie with the sticky fingers was none other than Bebe's client, Lacey Hunt.

Tatiana said she suspected Bebe had blackmailed the rising young movie star into becoming her client. Maybe Bebe knew about Lacey's shoplifting antics and was indeed blackmailing her. Maybe she was demanding more than just her patronage; maybe she was demanding money on the side.

And maybe Lacey, desperate to get out from under Bebe's oppressive thumb, was the one who wrung that wire around Bebe's neck.

"Is there something I can show you?"

I turned to see an eager saleslady at my side.

"No thanks. I've seen more than enough already."

Chapter 22

I headed out to the Neiman Marcus parking lot, my brain awash in images of Lacey Hunt stashing bibelots in her tote. I was so lost in my thoughts that it wasn't until I reached for my keys that I realized my car door was already open.

But that couldn't be. I was certain I'd locked it.

Damn it all. Someone had broken into my car!

What if they stole my auto registration? Or my radio? Or my emergency stash of M&M's?

But it was worse than that. Much worse.

When I got in the car, I saw something that made me break out in a cold sweat.

There, hanging from my rearview mirror, was a wire hanger—twisted into a noose!

It looked like I'd just received a death threat from the killer.

With trembling hands, I took it down and tossed it onto the passenger seat. My hands were still shaking as I put my key in the ignition.

Then, out of nowhere, I heard the roar of an engine and looked up to see a low-slung foreign sports car zooming toward the exit.

I suddenly flashed back to my last encounter with Miles Braddock in Bebe's studio—and the check I'd seen made out to Beverly Hills Maserati.

Was that Miles behind the wheel?

I had to find out. Wasting no time, I took off after him.

There was a short line of cars at the exit, and as I rolled up behind the exotic sports car, I saw that it was indeed a Maserati. The driver behind the wheel was a big guy—just like Miles. Then the driver's side window rolled down, and a beefy arm flicked off the ash from a cigar.

That clinched it. It was Miles, all right. He put that noose in my car. And I wasn't about to let him get away.

Luckily, there was plenty of traffic in Beverly Hills. Otherwise my pokey Corolla could never have kept up with him. But thanks to the cars glutting the streets, I was able to follow Miles as he wended his way toward Westwood, periodically flicking cigar ash from his window.

Finally he pulled up in front of an upscale sports club, where he got out and handed his keys to one of the white-uniformed valets. I couldn't quite make out his face. But I'd recognize that muscle-gone-to-pot build anywhere.

With no time to do my usual search for a free parking spot, I pulled up to the valets and tossed them my keys, racing into the sports club just in time to see Miles heading down a hallway.

I barreled past a Mr. Universe wannabe at the reception desk, who shouted:

"Hey, this club is for members only. Where do you think you're going?"

"To catch a killer!" I cried, scurrying across the lobby and down the hallway in search of Miles.

Sure enough, there he was, up ahead of me.

As I charged after him, I passed a janitor who cried out something to me in Spanish.

"Sorry!" I said, waving him off. "No hablo español."

By now, Miles had pushed open a door at the end of the hallway and headed inside.

Seconds, later, I was shoving my way past the same door.

At which point, a bit of a commotion broke out.

"Wrong room, lady!" someone yelled.

I looked around, and I realized I'd stumbled into the men's locker room.

So that's what the janitor had been trying to tell me.

All around me, guys were reaching for something to cover their privates. Others, not so shy, were happy to let it all hang out.

But I ignored them all (well, almost all—I'm only human), determined to nab Miles.

I soon spotted him from behind as he opened his locker door.

"Miles Braddock!" I called out. "I hereby make a citizen's arrest, charging you with the murder of your wife, Bebe Braddock!"

It was then that Miles turned around. And for the first time, I got a good look at his face.

Dammit! It wasn't Miles, but a cigar-chomping stranger.

"Gosh, I'm so sorry," I stammered. "I thought you were someone else."

"You can arrest me any time you want, sweetheart!" exclaimed one of the patrons in the locker room who hadn't bothered to cover up—a beer-bellied fellow with the most alarming man boobs.

I had no time to reject his nauseating offer. Because just

then two security guys showed up and grabbed me by my elbows, not so gently escorting me to the lobby, where, after taking down my name and address from my driver's license, they ejected me from the premises, warning me to never again darken their doorstep.

I slinked over to my Corolla, red-faced with shame. I had made an utter fool of myself in a room full of wealthy naked men—not to mention the Mr. Universe receptionist, who'd called after me on my way out:

"You need to work on your glutes!"

And as if all that weren't bad enough, I had to fork over thirteen dollars for valet parking.

Some days it just doesn't pay to get out of your I ♥ MY CAT sleepshirt.

Okay, so the guy I'd been following wasn't Miles and I'd just embarrassed myself big time in front of a bunch of naked strangers. But I couldn't deny the fact that someone, undoubtedly Bebe's killer, left that noose in my car.

Time to pay a visit to Detective Denzel Washington.

I fished his card from my purse and made my way over to his precinct, a concrete block of a building not far from the sports club in West L.A.

Inside the fluorescent-lit reception area, I waited to talk to the desk sergeant while an elderly lady in front of me insisted she'd been a victim of mail theft because she hadn't received a birthday card from her best friend, Eloise.

"Eloise and I have been friends since fourth grade in Minot, South Dakota, and she's never once missed a birthday. That card was stolen, all right. And I know who did it. That awful Mr. Engel across the street! He's had it in for me ever since Mr. Sniffles, my chihuahua, took the teensiest poop in his driveway.

"I insist on a thorough investigation!" she cried. "Tampering with the mail is a federal offense!"

The desk sergeant nodded wearily and suggested that she might want to contact Eloise to find out if she actually sent the card.

"Of course she sent the card! Eloise would never forget my birthday."

He continued to listen to her blather with the patience of a saint. Me, I wasn't so patient. I wanted to send her a birthday card myself, just to shut her up.

She finally stepped aside to fill out some paperwork, and at last it was my turn.

"Can I help you?" the sergeant asked.

I gave him my name and told him I needed to speak to Detective Washington immediately.

"I've got important evidence in the Bebe Braddock murder case." I held up the noose, stashed in one of the many eco-friendly reusable shopping bags I keep in the trunk of my car, always forgetting to actually bring one into a store.

He nodded and told me to take a seat while he put in a call to Detective Denzel, muttering something about a crazy lady. I couldn't tell if he meant me or the mail theft gal who was still painstakingly writing down the details of her missing birthday card.

Minutes later, Detective Washington came out to greet me in a rumpled white shirt, his tie loosened at the neck. He led me into a large room past a bunch of other cops to his workstation.

The nameplate on his desk read DENZEL G. WASHINGTON, and I couldn't help wondering if the G stood for George.

"You caught me at the end of my lunch break," he said, gesturing for me to take a seat across from him.

Indeed, I saw a McDonald's bag in his trash, a few remaining fries poking out of the bag.

I can never understand people who don't finish their fries. Don't they realize that if not properly composted, these fries emit noxious, high-calorie gases into the air? Now I have no hard evidence, but I'll bet a lot of global warming is caused by people like Denzel George Washington.

Save the planet! I felt like telling him. *Finish your fries!*

"Ms. Austen?"

Denzel was looking at me questioningly.

Oh dear. He'd asked me something, and I'd been so caught up in my internal rant about uneaten fries, I hadn't heard him.

"So where's that important piece of evidence?" he asked.

"Here!" I whipped out the noose from my shopping bag. "Someone broke into my car and left this hanging from my rearview mirror."

"I see," he said, frowning.

Reaching into his desk drawer, he took out a rubber glove and put it on before taking the noose from me and slipping it into a plastic evidence bag.

"I'll have it tested for fingerprints, but I suspect the only prints we'll find will be yours. Whoever left this in your car most likely wore gloves."

Gaak! Why the heck had I touched the darn thing with my bare hands? Why hadn't I used a tissue? You'd think I'd have learned my lesson after my whole fingerprints-on-the-murder-weapon fiasco.

"Who do you think might have done this?" he asked.

"Bebe's killer, of course. Trying to scare me off."

"Scare you off? From what?"

"I may have been nosing around," I confessed, "asking a few questions about the murder."

His brow furrowed in disapproval. As I've learned from past experience, the police don't exactly love it when you interfere in their murder investigations.

"Not very wise," he said. "Best leave the questioning to us, okay?"

"Absolutely," I lied.

"So what did you discover during this investigation of yours?"

I told him about Miles's affair with Anna, Tatiana's threat to get even with Bebe for stealing her clients, about the cut on Anna's hand, and Lacey possibly being blackmailed by Bebe. I didn't mention Heidi's wire horse, still grateful for my fabulous haircut and unwilling to throw her under the bus.

I was expecting Denzel to be taking copious notes, but he just nodded, as if nothing I said was news to him.

So much for my groundbreaking detective work.

"Once more, Ms. Austen, I urge you to leave the investigating to us. Homicide is serious business, and you don't want to find yourself on the wrong end of a murder weapon."

"Absolutely," I lied again, my fingers crossed firmly behind my back.

No way was I going to let go of this case, not until the real killer (and not yours truly) was locked up behind bars.

"One last word of advice," he added, as I got up to go.

"Yes?"

He gazed at me sternly.

"Stay out of men's locker rooms."

Damn. Those security goons had ratted me out to the cops.

I nodded, shamefaced, and hustled back to the reception area, where the elderly mail theft lady had found her missing birthday card.

"How about that?" she was saying to the desk sergeant. "It was here in my purse all along!"

At least her mystery had been solved.

Mine, I'm afraid, was far from over.

Chapter 23

In case you're wondering whatever happened to Justin, so was I. I hadn't heard from him in days. Which is why my heart did a little flip-flop when I checked my phone in my car and saw a text from him.

Justin:
Free tonight?

Inviting me out at the very last minute? An absolute No-No. No way could I possibly say yes.

Me:
Sure!!

Not only that, I added a happy face emoji.

Justin:
Great! My friend invited me to an art gallery opening. Pick you up at seven?

Me:
Perfect!

Justin:
Don't bother eating dinner. They're serving great hors d'oeuvres.

Good news indeed. Free chow—and Justin.

I couldn't wait to dig into both.

* * *

If truth be told, I'm not much of an art buff. (My idea of a creative masterpiece is a Ben & Jerry's hot fudge sundae.) But that night I was lost in fantasies of my exciting new life as an art aficionado, some day strolling through the Louvre arm in arm with Justin, sneaking smooches in deserted corridors.

I checked myself out in my full-length mirror, dressed in what I hoped was art gallery chic—skinny jeans, black turtleneck, dangly silver earrings, and my trusty Manolos.

Prozac, who'd ambled over to stand next to me, purred in approval.

Looking good, girl!

Needless to say, she was looking at herself.

Justin showed up at seven, scrumptious as ever, sporting his TEAM BEBE bomber jacket, dimple flashing.

He eyed me appreciatively and kissed me lightly on my lips, a feathery touch that sent shivers down my spine.

"Preview of coming attractions," he whispered.

This idyllic moment was shattered, however, when Prozac came hurtling over, wedging herself between us, batting her big green eyes at Justin, in full-tilt coquette mode.

Hello, handsome! Wanna spend the night feeding me bacon bits?

She clung to his ankles like a barnacle, but somehow I managed to wrench her away and deposit her on the sofa, only to be met by a chorus of indignant meows.

Which I promptly proceeded to ignore.

"Shall we?" I said, grabbing my purse and herding Justin out the door.

From the sofa, Pro lobbed me the royal stink eye.

I'll get you for this.

I had no doubt she would. I fully expected to find a hairball on my pillow that night.

But all I cared about at that moment was climbing behind Justin on his motorcycle and wrapping my arms around his scrumptiousity. By now, I was getting used to riding on the motorcycle and had only mild heart palpitations as we zoomed across town, weaving in and out of traffic.

Our destination was an art gallery on Santa Monica's Main Street, a strip of terminally hip restaurants and shops. Justin parked between two BMWs, and as we made our way to the gallery, I looked in the window of a bistro at a guy biting into a thick, juicy burger. It was all I could do not to run in and grab it out of his hands.

Frankly, I was starving.

I'd had nothing, absolutely nothing, to eat since lunch.

Not even a single Oreo. For once in my life, I'd reined myself in, saving my appetite for those delicious hors d'oeuvres Justin had promised.

The gallery turned out to be a large box of a space with walls painted a stark white. A sign in the window told us we'd arrived at FUN-TOPIA!

"This exhibit should be terrific," Justin was saying. "Very avant-garde, cutting-edge. Not your stuffy old traditional paintings."

The first thing I noticed when we walked inside was a sandbox full of Styrofoam peanuts. Next to that, some randomly tossed cardboard boxes. And beyond that, Ken and Barbie in miniature coffins.

If this was art, I was a marine biologist.

"So what do you think?" Justin asked with an eager smile.

"Never seen anything like it," I managed to say.

"C'mon," he said, grabbing me by the hand. "Let's check out my friend's work."

He led me toward the back of the gallery, past a skeleton at a keyboard (*Beethoven De-Composing*) and a replica of the Mona Lisa made out of jelly beans.

I actually liked the jelly bean Mona Lisa, although it had the unfortunate effect of reminding me just how hungry I was.

"Justin, sweetie!" a hoarse voice croaked out.

I turned to see a tall, painfully skinny woman in a flowy black caftan waving at Justin. With her chalky face, lank black hair, and blood-red lipstick, she looked like she'd just stepped out of an espisode of *The Munsters*.

"Welcome to Fun-topia, darling!" she rasped, throwing her bony arms around Justin. "So glad you made it."

"Great to see you, Tacoma," he said when she finally let him go. "Meet my friend Jaine."

Tacoma looked me up and down with a tepid smile, clearly writing me off as the artistic philistine that I was, and instantly turned her attention back to Justin, linking her arm in his.

"So what do you think?" she asked, gesturing to a bunch of empty wine bottles lying in a pile of dirt. "I call it *Planet of the Grapes*."

"Fascinating," Justin murmured.

Then she pointed to a series of pizza boxes glued together so they rose up from the floor in a slant.

"Guess what I call this one?"

"*The Leaning Tower of Pizza*?" I asked.

"No," she snapped with a withering glare. "*The Unbearable Lightness of Being*.

"And finally, my personal favorite." She pointed to a

jigsaw puzzle with a single piece missing. "This one I call *Despair*."

"Wow," Justin said, "these are blowing my mind."

Really? There went my fantasy of us touring the Louvre together.

While Justin and Tacoma were admiring the jigsaw puzzle, my eyes lingered on those pizza boxes, thinking how yummy a pizza would taste right then. Or better yet, that burger I'd seen on the way over. Where the heck were all those wonderful hors d'oeuvres Justin had talked about?

I looked around the gallery for signs of food, but saw nothing except for the jelly bean Mona Lisa. If the damn thing weren't shellacked together, I'd have been tempted to run over and eat her enigmatic smile.

Then, just as I was losing hope of ever finding anything edible, I spotted a waiter circulating with a tray of goodies at the far side of the gallery.

I willed him to come our way, but that didn't seem to be happening.

Meanwhile, Tacoma held Justin in a vise-like grip, trashing the other artists and gabbing about mutual friends.

I was just about to sprint across the room to the waiter when Tacoma said, "I heard Bebe Braddock got killed."

"Yeah," Justin said. "What a shocker, huh?"

"Not to me," Tacoma replied. "I knew it was happening."

What the what?

"I remember the night vividly. I was at the Brentwood Country Mart and ran into Heidi, Bebe's hair and makeup gal. Heidi was supposed to exhibit one of her pieces here tonight, but they didn't have room for it. Anyhow, as we were chatting about Bebe and what a ghastly woman she was, I suddenly sensed Bebe's life force being snuffed out of her. I'm psychic, you know. I get these insights all the time. And sure enough, the next morning, I saw on the news that Bebe had been killed the night before."

She continued blabbing about her psychic abilities and how they enriched her "art," but I'd stopped listening.

The waiter had made his way to our side of the gallery. Like a shot, I was at his side.

"Vegetarian lettuce wrap?" he asked, holding out a tray of the most paltry hors d'oeuvres west of a gulag.

How depressing, I thought, popping one in my mouth.

As I stood there chewing on my lettuce, still wishing I were biting into that juicy burger, I flashed back on what Tacoma said about running into Heidi in Brentwood the night of murder.

Hold on.

What the heck was Heidi doing in Brentwood? Heidi lived in the Fairfax district, miles away. And if you re-member, she said she'd been home all night, working on her vacuum cleaner giraffe. She'd lied about her alibi. Heidi wasn't home all night. For at least part of the night, she was at the Brentwood Country Mart, just a wire hanger's throw from Bebe's studio.

Over at her exhibit, Tacoma was still clinging to Justin, blathering about her psychic powers. "I can predict earth-quakes, you know," she was saying.

I didn't have the energy to join them, so I wandered aimlessly past "art" that looked like stuff dumped at the curb on garbage day—all the while on the alert for a pass-ing waiter. But the only food I saw were those jelly beans on the Mona Lisa.

I was *thisclose* to prying some loose when I spotted my salvation, over in a far corner of the gallery: A big beauti-ful vending machine!

In a flash, I bolted my way past the art lovers, praying

the machine would have something decent to eat. At a joint like this, it'd probably be filled with celery sticks.

But no, as I approached the machine, I saw it had actual candy inside. My eyes zeroed in on a Snickers bar for a dollar. I reached in my bag and pulled out my wallet. Damn. All I had was a ten, and the machine only accepted singles and quarters.

A quick check of my change purse yielded three quarters. Just one quarter more, that's all I needed. Frantically I rummaged around in the bottom of my bag and—miracle of miracles—along with a linty Life Saver and a petrified Tootsie Roll, I dug up a loose quarter.

Yahoo! Any second now, I'd be biting into my Snickers!

As I put the quarters in the slot, I could practically taste its chewy caramel melting in my mouth. But when I pressed the button for my candy, nothing happened. The Snickers stayed right where it was, snug in its little compartment.

Damn. I pressed the button again.

Still nothing. So I gave the machine a bang. But that Snickers wasn't budging.

By now, I was pretty darn mad. That cursed machine had eaten my four quarters.

Crazed with hunger, I banged even harder.

Still nothing.

A crowd had gathered around me, looking on with interest. Some of them were even giggling. I didn't see what was so funny about a defective vending machine.

"Darn machine is broken," I said, giving it a rather vicious kick.

At which point, Justin came hurrying to my side.

"Jaine, that isn't a working vending machine. It's one of the art installations."

Oh, hell. I was so darn embarrassed, I felt like burying myself in the dirt at *Planet of the Grapes*.

"I bet you're starving," Justin said, guiding me away from the tittering crowd. "The hors d'oeuvres aren't nearly as good as they were the last time I was here. What do you say we go down the street and grab a burger?"

"I don't think so. I've got a busy day tomorrow. I'd better go home and call it a night."

No, your eyes are not deceiving you. As hungry as I was, I really did say that. Looking around at the artsy young crowd, I realized that Justin and I came from two different worlds. I didn't belong with these hip twentysomethings. All I wanted was to go home and settle down in bed with Pro and a pint of Chunky Monkey.

"Of course," Justin said. "Let's go."

He put his arm around my waist to lead me out of the gallery. And the minute he touched me, I felt a tingle in my lady parts. Darn it all. Why did I have to be so attracted to this guy?

Outside, with his arm still around my waist, we walked down the street toward his motorcycle.

"So what did you think of the exhibit?" he asked.

"It was . . . um . . . very interesting."

"You lie. You hated it."

"Well, I liked the jelly bean Mona Lisa."

"Frankly," Justin said, "I thought most of it was pretty silly. It wasn't nearly as good as the exhibit I saw the last time I was here. And Tacoma can be a bit much."

Gee, maybe we did have something in common. Maybe our worlds were closer together than I'd thought.

"I feel bad about those hors d'oeuvres," he said. "I promised you a meal, and all you got was a fake vending machine. Are you sure you don't have time for a quick burger?"

He smiled down at me now, dimple flashing.

That's all it took.

"Okay," I said, practically melting in a puddle at his feet.

"With extra fries?" he asked, running his finger along my cheek.

"With extra fries," I nodded.

And then, right there in the middle of Main Street, he took my face in his hands and kissed me.

Now that was my idea of Fun-topia!

You've Got Mail

To: Jausten
From: Shoptillyoudrop
Subject: Wish Me Luck!

Wish me luck, sweetheart! The gals will be here soon for the book club, and I'm just hoping I can lead a discussion about a book I haven't actually read.

On a more positive note, the patio looks quite lovely—the perfect setting for our little gathering.

My whipped cream and fruit parfait looks positively elegant in my beautiful crystal parfait bowl. And I've got that yummy wine chilling for the spritzers. So at least the refreshments will be a success.

I warned Daddy not to barge in like he often does to "entertain" the ladies with his corny jokes, but thank heavens he's busy playing with some new gadget he bought online.

I'll write later to let you know how it went—

XOXO,
Mom

To: Jausten
From: DaddyO

Great news, Lambchop! My spy drone arrived this morning! Heading out to the driveway to give it a trial run. Before long, I'll be launching it into the stratosphere.

Isn't technology great?

Love 'n hugs from,
Daddy

To: Jausten
From: Shoptillyoudrop
Subject: Utter Disaster

Book club was an utter disaster. All because of Daddy.

It was going wonderfully well at first. It turns out I wasn't the only one who hadn't read the book. In fact, hardly any of the ladies managed to finish it. Most of them just Googled it or saw the movie. We all agreed that Audrey Hepburn looked fabulous in her period costumes and were soon happily sipping wine spritzers and chatting about our favorite Audrey Hepburn movies.

As I said, it was all going like a dream, one of our best book clubs ever, when I brought out the pièce de résistance, my whipped cream fruit parfait.

The gals oohed and aahed as I set the parfait bowl down on the table. Some of them even got out their cell phones to take pictures.

Then, just as I was about to scoop out the servings, we heard a loud buzzing noise in the sky, and suddenly what looked like a big metal bird came crashing down—right into the par-fait.

Fruit and whipped cream went flying everywhere. Poor Edna Lindstrom wound up with blueberry stains all over her new silk blouse.

The metal bird turned out to be the gadget Daddy was playing with, something called a drone that he bought to spy on Lydia Pinkus!

Honestly, I'm so mad I could spit!

XOXO,
Mom

PS. Thanks to that stupid drone, my parfait bowl now has a giant crack right down the middle.

To: Jausten
From: DaddyO
Subject: Not My Fault!

I suppose Mom wrote you about the little incident on the patio. Unfortunately I lost control of the drone, and it wound up nose-diving into her whipped cream and fresh fruit par-fait.

But it's not really my fault.

I blame it all on the faulty directions that came with the drone. Believe you me, I'm going to write an angry letter to their customer relations department.

First of all, it wasn't nearly as easy to operate as it looked online. I was standing out on our driveway for at least forty-five minutes before I was finally able to launch it. I tried to aim it out in the street, but the darn thing insisted on going its own way—up over the roof of our house to the back patio, where out of nowhere it stopped working and made its unfortunate descent into your mom's parfait.

Now it's clogged with whipped cream and berries, totally out of commission.

When Mom found out I'd bought the drone to spy on Lydia, she blew a gasket and made me promise to throw the drone straight in the trash.

Which I did. (It was broken, anyway.)

Now I'm off to Bed Bath & Beyond to buy her a new parfait bowl.

Love 'n hugs from,
Daddy

To: Jausten
From: DaddyO
Subject: You'll Never Guess

You'll never guess what just happened, Lambchop!

I was at Bed Bath & Beyond to get Mom that new parfait bowl and was browsing around, looking at an amazing combination-slicer-dicer-blender, when I happened to glance up and saw The Battle-Axe huddled in a corner near the upright vacuum cleaners, talking on her cell phone.

With lightning speed, I put on my aviator sunglasses, pulled down the brim of my baseball cap, and scurried over to a nearby aisle—just in time to hear her saying:

"Hideaway Motel? Thanks for returning my call. I'd like to reserve a room for next Friday. Room number twelve, the quiet room at the end of the motel. You have my credit card on file, my name is . . ."

Waaah, waaah, waaah! Mommy, I wanna cookie!

A little kid wailing in his stroller cut off the rest of the conversation, but I had all the info I needed. The Battle-Axe has made plans to meet The Flounder for an X-rated lovers' tryst. Little does she know, she's about to have an unexpected visitor.

Soon her secret love won't be a secret anymore!

Love 'n snuggles from,
Your crusading
Daddy

PS. I was so darn excited about Lydia's tryst, I forgot to buy the parfait bowl.

To: Jausten
From: Shoptillyoudrop
Subject: Impossible!

Daddy went to Bed Bath & Beyond to buy me a new parfait bowl and came back with a stupid slicer-dicer-blender instead.

The man is impossible!

XOXO,
Mom

Chapter 24

Fun-topia was all very well and good, but it wasn't getting me any closer to finding Bebe's killer.

(In case you're wondering, there was no dipsy doodle that night. After scarfing down burgers on Main Street, Justin and I returned to my duplex, where he took me in his arms and zapped me with a flurry of good-night kisses. But true to his promise to take things slowly, he tore himself away before things escalated to the mattress zone, leaving me dazed and panting at my front door.)

The next morning, I woke up determined to shelve all thoughts of Justin and focus on the murder.

I got momentarily distracted, however, when I opened my emails and saw that bombshell of a message from Daddy. Had he really heard Lydia Pinkus reserving a room for two at The Hideaway Motel? Could it be? Was Lydia Pinkus, TV's bastion of propriety, actually having an affair?

I reeled at the thought of "The Battle-Axe" tearing off her support hose in a moment of passion. But I couldn't go down that rabbit hole. Not with a pesky murder to solve.

I needed to talk with Lacey Hunt and find out if Bebe had been blackmailing her. Consulting the contact list Justin had given me, I put in a call to her.

If I was hoping to speak with the movie star in person, I was in for a disappointment. A brisk young woman named Petra answered the phone and informed me, in no uncertain terms, that Lacey had said all she was going to say about Bebe's murder to the police and that I did not have a snowball's chance in hell of chatting with her.

"Besides," she added, "Lacey's not even home today. She's at the studio, shooting her new movie."

Needless to say, she did not tell me which studio or what movie.

I hung up, dispirited, but still determined to track down the sticky-fingered star. I checked a few show biz industry websites for any mention of Lacey's new movie but came up empty-handed.

Then inspiration struck.

Weren't celebs always posting pictures of themselves on Instagram, doing fun things in fab locations, eager to keep their presence alive on social media?

Sure enough, there on her Instagram page was a picture of Lacey in a stylist's chair, her hair in rollers, looking prettier than any woman has a right to look without makeup.

"Here I am," she'd written, "at Spectacular Studios, prepping for my new movie, *Love Is in the Air.*"

You know, of course, there's no actual Spectacular Studios. It's a name I made up to protect the innocent (namely, *moi*) from a lawsuit. The last thing I needed was a pack of Spectacular lawyers coming after me, pressing charges for stealing that moose head.

But I'm getting ahead of myself. More about the moose head later.

Let's get back to Lacey. Now that I knew where she was, I had to figure out a way to get onto the studio lot.

No way would the guards at the gate let me in without a pass.

Somehow I'd have to sneak in. But how?

Simple! I'd take the famous Spectacular Studios tram ride, and when no one was looking, I'd hop off the tram and scout around until I found the soundstage for *Love Is in the Air*.

I patted myself on the back for being so clever.

After a fortifying cinnamon raisin bagel, I bid Prozac farewell and tooled over to Spectacular's sprawling home in Burbank. And I do mean sprawling. It took me forever just to find the visitors' parking structure and snag a space for my Corolla, snaking my way up to what seemed like the 312th level.

Elbowing my way past the tourists at Spectacular's theme park, I arrived at the ticketing area for the studio tour, where I was in for a most unpleasant shock.

Who knew studio tours were so expensive? In a stunning blow to my Mastercard, I forked over an obscene amount of money for a ticket, then got on line to wait for a tram.

On a weekday morning at eleven there wasn't too much of a crowd, so I only had to wait about ten minutes—ten minutes that seemed like decades, however, due to the tyke in front of me who kept hollering at the top of his lungs, "Where's Mickey Mouse?" No matter how many times his parents explained that they weren't at Disneyland, the kid kept wailing for Mickey.

Finally, my eardrums throbbing, we were led onto a two-car, open-air tram. There I caught my first break, grabbing a seat at the very back of the second car, out of sight of the tour guide in the first car.

Which meant I could hop off the tram without him noticing me. Even better, the tram wasn't full, so I had the whole back row to myself. I hunkered down next to the outside guardrail, so it would be easy peasy to jump over to freedom when the tram stopped to visit an attraction.

Then, just when I thought the tram had finished loading, a last minute passenger came rushing on, a ruddy-cheeked, middle-aged gal in capri pants and flip-flops—her glasses hanging from a chain around her neck, a tabloid newspaper clutched in her hand.

I watched in dismay as she walked down the aisle past several empty seats and plopped herself right next to me in the back row. Can you believe it? The whole row was empty, and she had to sit next to me!

"Oh my!" she exclaimed. "Isn't this exciting! I heard Bratt Pitt is shooting a movie here! Isn't he gorgeous?" She pointed to a picture of Brad on the cover of her tabloid, breaking up with Jennifer Aniston for the umpteenth time. "I drove all the way up from Whittier, hoping to see him."

By this point, the guardrails had been lowered into place, our genial tour guide, Sean, had welcomed us aboard, and we were off and running.

Sean was yakking about the fun to come, his face visible on a monitor at the front of the tram. The little kid from the ticket line was still screaming for Mickey Mouse. And my seatmate, Shirley—by now, we were on a first name basis—was still on a roll about Brad.

"I love my husband, of course," Shirley was saying, "but I've had a mad crush on Brad ever since I first saw him in *Thelma and Louise*. I even called in sick at work, hoping to catch a glimpse of him today. I'm a dental hygienist, you know. Seventeen years with Dr. William Schroeder, the 'Crown Prince' of Whittier. Lord, he's got great teeth—not Dr. Schroeder, his teeth are a mess. But Brad, just look at that smile!"

She beamed down at the tabloid picture of Brad and shook her head in dismay.

"All those years with Angelina. I knew it would never last. She's just not right for him. He should have never left Jen."

By now, she was practically sitting on my lap. How was I ever going to make my escape? I could only hope she'd pry herself away from me to look at an attraction on the other side of the tram.

Just my lousy luck, the first several stops were on my side of the tram, with everyone looking in my direction. What if all the stops were on my side? Why, oh why, had I chosen this stupid seat?

But at last we came to an exhibit on the other side of the tram—a man-made body of water where, Sean informed us, a terrifying sea monster would soon be rearing its ugly head.

And sure enough, seconds later, a scaly green creature came bubbling up from the water, spewing flames with a deafening roar. I was waiting for Shirley to rush to the other side of the tram to get a better look, but she didn't move a muscle.

"Who cares about a silly old sea monster?" she said, gazing fondly at the photo of Brad in her lap.

Gaak! I couldn't let this opportunity slip through my fingers. Who knew when or if I'd get another chance to break away?

Then, glancing down at Shirley's tabloid, I got an idea.

"Look!" I cried. "It's Brad Pitt!"

"Where?" Shirley asked, looking around frantically.

"Over there!" I pointed to the other side of the tram. "Scoot on over, and I'm sure you'll see him."

And praise be, she was up like a shot, her head hanging out the other side of the tram.

This was it, the moment I'd been waiting for. Wasting no time, I hurled myself over the guardrail and jumped down to freedom. Scrambling to my feet, I started sprinting down a dusty dirt road. I thought I heard Shirley shouting, but it was hard to be sure over the sea monster's roar and the kid still wailing for Mickey Mouse. After a while, I shored up my courage and glanced backward, fully expecting to see Sean hot on my heels. But the tram had long since headed off to its next destination.

It looked like I was safe for now.

Soon I emerged onto the studio back lot, dotted with bungalow-style offices and huge soundstages.

I pulled my hair into a hasty ponytail and stowed the sweater I'd been wearing in my tote, hoping to obliterate any resemblance to the woman who'd just bolted from a tour tram.

Walking along, trying my best to look like I actually belonged on the lot, I passed a bunch of guys in scruffy jeans and T-shirts, their faces gaunt and hollow-eyed.

(Comedy writers, no doubt.)

They barely glanced at me.

And they weren't the only ones who seemed to think I worked there. Several other people passed me by without incident, some of whom even nodded hello.

I was beginning to think I was going to get away with this crazy plan of mine when I looked up and saw a steely-eyed security guard in a golf cart heading straight toward me.

Dammit. Shirley had undoubtedly opened her big blabbity mouth and reported me missing to Sean, who'd sicced the studio police on me.

My ponytail wasn't fooling the goon in the golf cart.

Any minute now, I was about to be hauled off to studio jail for illegal trespassing!

Chapter 25

In a panic, I dashed into the nearest bungalow.

"It's about time!" cried a harried young woman at the reception desk. "I thought you'd never get here." Then she shouted out to someone in a back room. "The new temp just showed up.

"Take this to Stage Five right now," the receptionist said. "They're waiting for it."

With that, she reached behind her desk and pulled out a fake, but very hairy, moose head.

Now the honorable thing would have been to tell her the truth, that I was not the new temp, but an escapee from a tour tram. But I could not afford to be honorable. Not with that security guard hot on my trail.

So I grabbed the moose head and said, "I'm on it."

What better way to look legit than carrying around a giant prop?

"Where's Stage Five?" I asked before heading out the door.

"It's three stages down on your left. And hurry!"

I opened the door, praying I wouldn't find the security guard waiting for me and breathed a sigh of relief when I saw he was gone.

So off I went with the moose head in my arms, hopefully obscuring any glimpse of my face. When I saw Stage Five on my left, I walked straight past it. No way was I giving up my camouflage.

I wandered around for what seemed like centuries, hauling that damn moose head. Yes, it was a great cover-up, but the thing was heavy, and its molting hair reeked of mothballs and sweat.

At last, I came across a soundstage where a poster out front informed me they were shooting Lacey's movie, *Love Is in the Air*.

I dumped the moose head behind a trash can and headed for a bunch of trailers parked nearby, sending profuse thanks to the studio gods when I found one with Lacey's name on it.

Then I knocked on the door, hoping I wasn't smelling too much of Eau de Moose.

"Come in," a soft voice called out.

Walking up the steps into the trailer, I saw Lacey on a sofa, her tiny bod wrapped in a terry robe, knitting what looked like an argyle sweater, a script splayed out beside her.

"Can I help you?" she asked.

I remembered what Petra, her assistant, said about Lacey refusing to talk about Bebe's murder. Luckily, traipsing across the studio lot had given me plenty of time to come up with a clever plan to avoid getting booted out of her trailer.

But before I could launch my plan, Lacey said, "Wait a minute. Don't I know you?"

Damn. What if she remembered me from Bebe's studio? My plan would never work if she knew my real identity.

"I don't think so," I said. "I'm Detective Connie Monroe. From Neiman Marcus Security."

I quickly flashed the USDA meat inspector's badge I'd

bought years ago at a flea market and saved for moments just like this.

Most people don't look at it closely, and Lacey was no exception.

Her face paled beneath her freckles.

"I was afraid something like this would happen some day," she groaned, abandoning her knitting and crumpling into a ball on her sofa.

"According to our security tapes," I said, "you were captured on camera shoplifting a scarf and a bracelet."

"I'm so sorry!" she wailed. "I promise I'll pay you back for the scarf. And the bracelet. And everything else I've taken."

Everything else? Looked like our perky young movie star had been on quite a shoplifting spree.

"I don't know why I do it, why I risk my career for things I can easily pay for. I'm such a fool!" she said, tears streaming down her cheeks.

"Don't worry. As long as you make restitution, we're all good."

But the waterworks kept coming, her body wracked with sobs. She was making such a racket, I was afraid a security guard would come bursting in to see what all the fuss way about.

"Look," I said, in a desperate effort to shut her up, "I'm not really with Neiman Marcus."

"What?" She looked up at me, her eyes red-rimmed from all those tears.

"You were right. We have met before, at Bebe's studio when she was giving me a makeover."

"I thought you looked familiar."

"I'm the one who discovered Bebe's body, and the police think I may have killed her. So I'm trying to clear my name. Tatiana Rogers told me she thought Bebe had black-mailed you into becoming her client. And then the other day, at Neiman's, I saw you stealing that scarf and the bracelet. So I came to find out if Bebe really was blackmailing you."

"Yes," she sighed, "that miserable woman hired a detective to follow me and get dirt on me. The guy saw me stealing a lipstick from CVS. And once Bebe found out about my little 'problem,' she threatened to tell the world unless I became her client."

So Lacey Hunt had a motive to kill Bebe.

A very compelling motive indeed.

As if reading my thoughts, she cried out, "But I swear I didn't kill her. Like I told the police, I was shooting on location in Westwood the night Bebe was killed. You can ask anybody on the crew. They'll tell you. I was there all night."

As much as I hated to lose a suspect, I believed her. Especially with a bunch of witnesses ready to vouch for her whereabouts the night of the murder.

"You've got to promise you won't tell a soul about my shoplifting," she begged.

"Only if you promise to see a therapist."

"Yes, of course," she said, nodding earnestly.

At which point, a sprightly young gal in jeans and a baseball cap came bounding up the steps into the trailer, holding a skein of yarn.

"Hi, Lacey. I brought you the yarn you wanted."

"Thanks, Petra," Lacey mumbled.

This had to be Petra, Lacey's guard dog of an assistant.

"My gosh!" Petra said, seeing Lacey's tear-stained face. "What's wrong?"

"Just a bit of bad news," Lacey replied with a rueful

smile. "But everything's all right now, isn't it?" she asked, turning to me.

"Yes, everything's fine," I assured her, heading down the steps of the trailer.

Fine for Lacey, maybe. Not so much for me.

As far as I knew, I was still a prominent blip on the LAPD's radarscope—not to mention a fugitive from justice here on the hallowed grounds of Spectacular Studios.

By the time I left Lacey, I wanted nothing more than to hurry home and soak my aching muscles in a nice hot bath.

But I couldn't leave yet.

Eager to expunge "moose head thief" from my résumé, I retrieved the smelly prop from behind the trash can where I'd stashed it and started the long trek back to Stage Five.

When I finally got there, the stage door was shut. Either they were busy shooting, or they'd shut down production for the day due to a missing moose head. Whatever the reason, I dropped my hairy companion at the stage door and ran as fast as I could.

I would have preferred running in the general direction of the visitors' parking lot, but I had no idea where that was.

I wandered around, lost in a sea of hulking soundstages and standing sets, wondering if I'd ever make it out alive, visions of my decaying corpse being discovered behind the false front of the saloon on Wild West Street.

Then a horn started honking behind me.

"Jaine Austen!" I heard a woman's voice call out. "Stop this minute!"

Damn. It had to be a security guard. They'd tracked me down at last.

I turned to see—not a security guard—but Heidi, my favorite haircutter, sitting behind the wheel of the cart, clad in her baggy overalls.

Never in my life had I been so relieved to see anyone. (Except possibly the delivery guy from my Fudge of the Month Club.)

"What're you doing here?" Heidi asked.

"It's a long story," I said, launching into the saga of how I'd escaped from the tour tram to question Lacey about Bebe's murder.

"No!" Heidi cried. "I heard about someone jumping the tram. Everyone was talking about it at the commissary. That was you?"

I nodded shamefully.

"I couldn't think of any other way to get onto the lot."

"If I'd only known," Heidi said, "I would've gotten you a pass."

"Anyhow, I'm dying to get out of here, but I have no idea where to find the visitors' parking lot."

"No problem. Hop on, and I'll take you."

I sank down next to her in the golf cart and listened as she chattered about how much she loved her new gig, styling eighteenth-century wigs for a period romance.

"So many curls! So little time!"

I was nestled in the cart, thrilled at the prospect of being reunited with my Corolla, when I remembered what Tacoma said at Fun-topia, about seeing Heidi at the Brentwood Country Mart the night of Bebe's murder.

I needed to ask Heidi about this, but I couldn't risk getting kicked out of the cart. So I waited until she'd pulled up to the parking lot entrance before finally broaching the subject.

"It's been so great seeing you," she said, giving me a hug. "I still have fond memories of us throwing darts at Bebe's poster."

"Yes, that was fun," I said, climbing down from the cart. "Thanks so much for the lift."

"De nada," she said, waving away my thanks.

But she wasn't rid of me yet.

"Before I go, there's something I want to ask you. I happened to run into a gal named Tacoma the other night, an artist pal of yours."

"Tacoma?" Heidi said, rolling her eyes. "She's quite a character. And I wouldn't exactly call her a pal. More like an acquaintance. A distant acquaintance."

"Anyhow," I plowed ahead, "Tacoma mentioned seeing you at the Brentwood Country Mart the night of Bebe's murder."

At this, Heidi's smile stiffened.

"Yeah, I was there. I went to pick up some cheese for a dinner party I was throwing the next night. What about it?"

"Nothing, really. It's just that you told me you were home all night."

"I was, mostly. I just ran out to get the cheese."

"But it's quite a drive from Fairfax to Brentwood, isn't it?"

Now all traces of her smile had vanished.

"What are you implying? That I popped by Bebe's studio to strangle her after I bought my cheese?"

"No, of course not," I lied. "I was just wondering, that's all."

"The Brentwood Country Mart has a Stilton cheese I really like. I drove out to get it, making zero stops along the way. I barely even hit a red light. I wasn't anywhere near Bebe's studio that night. Believe me, or don't believe me. I don't really care."

With that, she put the golf cart in gear and was off like a shot, no doubt cursing herself for having given me a lift.

I plodded back to my Corolla, wondering if Heidi could possibly be the killer.

One thing was for sure: There'd be no more freebie haircuts in my future.

Chapter 26

I stopped off at the supermarket on the way home for staples (Chunky Monkey and Pop-Tarts), as well as a couple of Lean Cuisine dinners—vowing not to eat them both in one sitting, as I usually do.

At the checkout counter, I grabbed a copy of *People* magazine's Sexiest Man Alive issue (my vote was for Justin), which I planned to read soaking in the tub.

Back at my apartment, I found Prozac snoring on the sofa, exhausted after a romp with her catnip mouse, which lay battered at her feet.

The minute she heard me come in, however, she was up like a shot, leaping onto the dining room table and parking herself next to my computer, yowling at the top of her lungs.

In the past, her yowling could mean only one thing: "Feed me!"

But now, if she was sitting next to my computer, it meant she wanted to watch the video of The Cat Who Saved a Toddler's Life.

Ever since that dratted video showed up online, she'd been obsessed with it, binge-watching it over and over again, never tiring of seeing herself on screen, thumping her tail in ecstasy.

With a sigh, I dumped my groceries on the kitchen counter and clicked on the video.

As she swooned over own image, I ran to the kitchen and barely got my groceries in the freezer before the video ended and she began yowling for me to play it again.

"That's enough," I said after playing the video eight times. "We're done here."

With that, I pried her from the screen and deposited her back on the sofa.

"It's not all about you, young lady," I scolded, plopping down beside her. "You won't believe what a ghastly day I had, escaping from the Spectacular Studios tram and hiding from security guards, traipsing miles across the studio lot with a stinky moose head—only to find out that Lacey isn't the killer, after all."

She gazed up at me with limpid green eyes.

You know what'll make you feel better? Scratching my back for the next twenty minutes.

Which, I'm ashamed to admit, is exactly what I did. And the thing is, she was right. It did make me feel better, kneading her silky fur, feeling the steady thrum of her purrs.

What can I say? I love the little devil.

Finally, when she was sound asleep, probably dreaming of herself as *People*'s Sexiest Cat Alive, I hauled myself from the sofa and started running the water for my long-awaited soak in the tub.

Minutes later, I was up to my neck in strawberry-scented bubbles, a glass of chardonnay and *People* magazine on the rim of the tub to keep me company.

I was flipping through celebrity breakups and makeups, facelifts and feuds, ogling the sexiest man alive (I was still voting for Justin), when I came across an article about Lacey Hunt, headlined NEW STAR SHINES IN HOLLYWOOD.

It was the usual pap about a fresh-faced kid growing up

in the Midwest, discovering acting in her high school drama club, moving to L.A., waiting tables and making the audition rounds until she eventually got discovered in a breakout part in an indie movie. There was some blather about her romance with an onscreen co-star, their subsequent breakup (see Makeups and Breakups, above), about life in her cozy three-million-dollar Santa Monica "farmhouse," where she loved cuddling with her cat and knitting—the hobby that kept her occupied during the many breaks on a movie shoot, where it can take hours to set up a single scene. Her other hobbies included yoga, Pilates, and pickleball. Finally, she confessed to being a dedicated shopaholic. "I love shopping of any kind," she gushed.

Yeah, right. Especially if she didn't have to pay for it.

By the time the article wrapped up, with a well-placed plug for her upcoming movie, I was more than ready move on to some Before and After facelift photos.

Eventually, tired of empty fluff, I tossed the magazine aside and lay back in the tub to think about more weighty matters: namely, what I was going to have for dinner. It was a toss-up between Chinese, pizza, and Lean Cuisine—with Lean Cuisine coming in a distant third. In the end, as tempted as I was by pizza's gooey globs of cheese, I opted for the comforting warmth of wonton soup and shrimp with lobster sauce.

Which, I can assure you, was quite comforting indeed.

It wasn't until I was in bed later that night, drifting off to sleep, that I sat up with a jolt, remembering something Lacey said in that *People* story: how she knitted to pass the time on movie sets, where it could take hours to set up a scene.

Lacey may have been on location in her trailer the night of the murder, but who's to say she didn't slip out and zip over to Brentwood during one of the interminable breaks to wring Bebe's neck? With the crew busy, it was quite possible no one had noticed her leave. Especially if she wore a baseball cap and jeans like her assistant Petra. Both gals were petite; Lacey could have easily been mistaken for Petra going out to run an errand for her movie star boss.

It looked like Lacey Hunt's airtight alibi had sprung a leak.

And back she went on my suspect list, knitting needles and all.

Chapter 27

Okay, Cocoa Puffs fans. The moment you've been waiting for—time for me to get back my CUCKOO FOR COCOA PUFFS T-shirt!

If you recall (and extra credit for those of you who do), Justin had given the T-shirt to Felipe, the gardener, who in turn had given it to his niece, Gloria, whose thieving roommate, Cindy, had stolen it when she moved out of their house. Gloria had no idea where Cindy was, only that she wrestled in Jello every other Sunday at the Sugar Shack, a dive bar in Redondo Beach.

So the next day, a glorious Sunday with cotton ball clouds scudding across a neon blue sky, I put Bebe's murder on hold and set out to retrieve my treasured tee.

The Sugar Shack turned out to be one of those "eat here at your own risk" joints a few blocks from the beach, packed with twentysomething surfer dudes swilling beer and watching ESPN on big-screen TVs.

A banner strung over the bar announced: JELLO WREST-LING AT 3 PM. TWO HUNDRED DOLLARS GRAND PRIZE MONEY.

I'd checked out the event online and got there fifteen minutes early so I'd have time to talk with Cindy before the fight began.

Seeing no sign of Jello anywhere, I asked the bartender where the wrestling was taking place.

"Out in the patio," he said, nodding toward the back of the bar.

I zigzagged my way past scarred wooden tables, the floor sticky beneath my feet, out onto a cement patio, where more revelers sat swilling booze at wooden benches.

At the far end of the patio, a bunch of bikini-clad beach bunnies with fab bodies and serious boobage were milling around a vat of what turned out to be lime-green Jello.

I picked out Cindy right away, due to my finely tuned powers of perception—and the fact that she was wearing my CUCKOO FOR COCOA PUFFS tee.

Unlike the beach bunnies, Cindy was a towering blonde with Brunhilda braids, bulging muscles, and biceps of steel.

(Think Godzilla in a sports bra.)

As I approached, I heard her screaming into her cell phone.

"What do you mean, you can't make it? So what if you've got food poisoning? Take a Tums!"

She clicked off the phone in disgust, not the happiest of campers. I sensed this might not be the best time to chat with her, but I was desperate to get my tee.

"Hi, there!" I chirped, with my brightest smile.

"What the hell do you want?" she grunted in reply.

"The CUCKOO FOR COCOA PUFFS T-shirt you're wearing. I'm the rightful owner of that shirt." Trying to be as diplomatic as possible, I added, "Your ex-roommate Gloria told me you must've accidentally taken it when you moved out. So I'm sure you won't mind giving it back to me."

At which point, the bar's manager, a deeply tanned man in a Hawaiian shirt, came over to the Jello vat and announced, "Ten minutes till fight time, ladies."

"Sure, I'll give you your T-shirt," Cindy said to me when he'd gone.

"Great!"

She was so much more reasonable than I thought she'd be.

"But only if you wrestle in the Jello with me."

"What??"

"The gal I'm supposed to fight can't make it because of some stupid food poisoning, and I want to win that two hundred bucks prize money."

"But I'm in no shape to fight someone like you."

"Ya think?" she said, eyeing my body and clearly finding it wanting. "No worries, though. I'll go easy on you. Just moan and groan and pretend I'm beating the stuffing out of you. I promise I won't hurt you."

"But I'm not dressed for the fight," I said, pointing to the skinny jeans and blouse I was wearing.

"No problem."

She took me by the hand led me back into the bar.

"Hey, Tony," she said to the guy in the Hawaiian shirt, "you got any clothes in your lost-and-found locker she can wrestle in?"

"No bikinis!" I piped up.

(The only one who gets to see my body in broad daylight is my gynecologist.)

Tony looked me over—like Cindy, none too impressed—and headed off down a corridor. Soon he was back with a pair of men's swim trunks and a beer-stained T-shirt.

At least I hoped it was beer.

"Go put these on," Cindy said, shoving me in the direction of the ladies' room, a filthy hole, certain to have been graded Z by the Health Department.

Gingerly, I began changing into my fighting togs, hoping to avoid any communicable diseases and wondering what sort of low-life dufus lost his swim trunks at a bar.

But on the plus side, at least the trunks covered my thighs.

On my way out of the ladies' room, I ran into a beach bunny, hobbling along on crutches.

"I hear you're wrestling Cindy today," she said to me.

"That's right."

"Watch out. She fights dirty. I wrestled with her a couple of weeks ago and wound up with these," she said, nodding at her crutches.

I gulped in dismay, but reminded myself of Cindy's promise to go easy on me.

By now, most of the beer-swilling surfer dudes had left the bar and gathered around the Jello vat in the patio, where Tony stood, beaming.

"Welcome, everybody," he said, "to the Sugar Shack's Jello wrestling contest, featuring some of the world's most sexy-licious beach bods!"

The audience hooted in approval.

Nobody was going to win any Political Correctness awards in this crowd.

"Remember the rules," Tony said. "Three matches. Three minutes each. Audience votes on the final winner."

The first two wrestlers got in the vat, and instantly my fears were dispelled. These gals weren't wrestling, only pretending to tackle each other, assuming positions usually seen on a porno site, showing off their boobage and booties whenever possible.

Clearly I had nothing to worry about. Cindy would pretend to tackle me, and I'd pretend to be overwhelmed, and before long, I'd be sailing off into the sunset with my beloved COCOA PUFFS tee.

As we waited our turn, Cindy proceeded to badmouth

the other contestants, pointing out whose boobs and butts had been surgically enhanced.

Now the second team stepped into the vat, where, after a few moments of Jello tossing and sex posing, a contestant named Brandi "accidentally" lost her bikini top, sending the crowd roaring with gleeful lust.

"Attention-grabbing slut," Cindy muttered through clenched teeth.

Eventually Brandi retrieved her bikini top, and it was our turn to frolic in the Jello.

Tony stepped up to announce us.

"And now, going up against Cindy 'The Bulldozer' Bukowski . . ."

The bulldozer? Gulp. I didn't like the sound of that.

". . . is newcomer Eleanor Roosevelt."

You didn't think I was going to use my real name, did you? I had a reputation to protect. Besides, I figured none of these bozos even knew who Eleanor Roosevelt was.

Cindy and I stepped into the vat of Jello, Cindy's jaw clenched, a most terrifying glint in her eyes.

Suddenly I felt like a poodle in a dogfight.

"You're going to go easy on me, right?" I whispered.

Wrong!

Before I knew it, she was shoving me down on my fanny and pelting me with Jello, then hauling me up only to shove me down again.

For one of the few times in my life, I was grateful for the extra padding in my tush.

Three minutes didn't seem very long when Tony was explaining the rules of the game, but now, with Cindy yanking me around the pool by my hair, it seemed like an eternity.

Some of the more sensitive bozos in the crowd, feeling sorry for me, called out, "Go, Eleanor, go!"

But I was incapable of putting up a fight, simply counting the seconds till this nightmare was over. As I was pulling myself up from the goo for about the fifth time and thinking things couldn't possibly get any worse, I saw Cindy charging at me, head bent, like a bull. The next thing I knew, she was head-butting me in my tummy.

Once again, I was grateful for my extra padding, but even so, I felt like I'd just been hit by a battering ram. Crumpling to my knees and gasping for air, I watched as Cindy strutted around the Jello vat, crying "I win! I win!"

But, in fact, she did not win.

When it was time for the guys to vote, Brandi won by a landslide. Even I got more applause than Cindy. Which seemed to irk her no end.

Flicking Jello off her massive biceps, Cindy grumbled about her loss, claiming the contest had been rigged.

None too happy myself, I said, "You told me you weren't going to hurt me. You lied."

"Of course, I lied."

"But why? You didn't have to hit me so hard; you would've beat me anyway."

"Yeah, but then it wouldn't have been any fun," she smirked.

Okay, this bimbo had just crossed a line. I could feel my blood starting to boil.

"I wrestled you, Cindy. Now I want my T-shirt."

I reached for the tee where she'd tossed it on the ground, but before I could grab it, she snatched it up.

"Forget about it," she said, still smirking that irritating smirk of hers. "I changed my mind. I'm keeping it. Just try to get it," she added, waving it in front of me.

That did it. Something within me snapped. This ghastly woman had mauled me and shoved Jello into every orifice on my body. She was a liar and a bully.

Now it was my turn to play the role of El Toro.

Head bent, I charged at her gut and landed with a most satisfying thump.

"Oof!" she cried, stumbling to the ground.

Wasting no time, I grabbed my COCOA PUFFS tee.

"You lose!" I said, waving the tee in victory for about a tenth of nanosecond before I saw her scrambling to her feet.

Snatching my jeans and blouse, I was off like a shot, but she was a lot faster than me. She would've caught up with me for sure, if that darling woman with the crutches hadn't shoved her crutch in Cindy's path, sending her sprawling.

And so, at long last reunited with my CUCKOO FOR COCOA PUFFS tee, I sprinted back to my Corolla—my heart full of joy, my lungs full of sea air, and my ears full of lime Jello.

Chapter 28

It took me three rounds with my shampoo bottle before I finally got rid of the Jello in my hair. And don't get me started on the rest of my body. I practically needed exploratory surgery to get rid of the stuff lodged in my various nooks and crannies.

I'd finally scrubbed away what I hoped was the last shard of Jello and climbed into my sweats when the phone rang.

"Jaine, sweetie." Tatiana Rogers's voice came sailing across the line.

I wondered why the stylist on the skids was calling. Maybe she had another lead for me. Her last tip about Lacey Hunt as a possible blackmail victim proved to be quite a gold mine.

But no, she had no leads to offer. It turned out to be a sales call.

"I've found the most delicious dress for you," she cooed. "A stunning black cocktail number in your size."

"Really, Tatiana, I can't afford your prices."

"I know, darling. That's why I'm prepared to let this treasure go for just fifty dollars!"

Underneath her cooing, I could hear a note of desperation in her voice.

My heart went out to her. She must have been really struggling to make ends meet. Besides, tomorrow night was that charity gala honoring Prozac, and I could use a new dress to wear.

"Won't you come have a look at it?" she pleaded. "I know you're going to love it."

"Okay, sure."

And so the next day I tootled out to Tatiana's place in the Valley. She came to the door dressed once again in a kimono, a frothy pink cocktail in her hand.

"Entrez, entrez!" she said, waving me inside with a flourish. "Strawberry daiquiri?" She held out her drink for my inspection. "They're marvelously healthy. All that fiber from the strawberries!"

"Thanks, but I'm good."

"Okay, let me find the dress for you."

Reluctantly she put her drink down on a wobbly end table and began rifling through the clothing rack that took up so much space in her tiny living room.

I remembered the sleazy leopard-print number she showed me the last time I was there. I wasn't betting the rent that this new offering would be any better, and so I was pleasantly surprised when she cried "Voilà!" and showed me her find: a tasteful little black dress with sexy spaghetti straps, fitted at the bust, flaring out into a flattering A-line skirt.

"A bargain," she said, "at only seventy five-dollars!"

"On the phone you said it was fifty."

"Did I? I don't recall saying that. Oh, well. We can always negotiate a price later."

Talk about your bait and switch.

"Why don't you try it on in here?" she said, leading me to her bedroom, a cramped shoebox of a room with an antique brass bed barely visible under a mountain of clothing. Clothes were strewn everywhere—on the bed, the floor, the dresser. The place looked like Nordstrom Rack after a tornado.

"Excuse the mess," she said. "It's the maid's day off."

Oh, please. The last time this place saw a maid, I was in diapers.

"I'll give you some privacy while you change."

Thank heavens she wouldn't be sticking around to ogle my cellulite.

As she handed me the dress, her cell phone rang. She reached into the pocket of her kimono to retrieve it, her eyes lighting up when she looked at the screen.

Eagerly she accepted the call.

"Lacey, darling!" she cried. "How marvelous to hear from you! Of course I'm available," she said as she tripped back out to the living room, practically walking on air. "I can't wait to get started."

It looked like Tatiana was about to be reunited with her treasured client.

Alone at last, I got undressed and slipped on the little black dress. When I checked myself out in the mirror on Tatiana's closet door, I was thrilled with what I saw, especially the way this clever little dress camouflaged my dreaded hip-thigh zone.

I twirled around, thinking how much fun it would be to wear this on a date with Justin, and melted at the thought of him sliding the spaghetti straps off my shoulders.

Wrenching myself from what was turning out to be quite a steamy daydream, I changed back into my clothes.

I was definitely going to spring for fifty (or even seventy-five) bucks and buy the dress. As I reached down to pick it up from the bed, something peeking out from the clutter caught my eye: A patch of bright red leather. Unearthing it from a pile of stretched-out bras, I saw it was a handbag, its supple leather trimmed with gold.

Something about the bag looked familiar; I was certain I'd seen it before. And then I remembered. It was the same red Birkin bag I'd seen at Bebe's studio, the day Tatiana came barging in, furious with Bebe for stealing Lacey away from her. I remembered Tatiana's rant about giving the bag to Bebe, only to have Bebe repay her by walking away with half her clients.

I snapped it open, and sure enough, there was Bebe's name embroidered on the bag's lining.

And it was at that exact moment that Tatiana came sailing into the bedroom, her kimono billowing out behind her.

"Fabulous news!" she gushed. "Lacey's signed on with me again!"

The bubble of joy she'd been riding on burst, however, when she saw the Birkin bag in my hands.

"What the hell are you doing with that?" she asked, whisking it away from me.

"I was just about to ask you the same question. This bag belonged to Bebe. Her name's embroidered inside. What's it doing here in your bedroom?"

Her eyes darted around the room, as if hoping to find an answer somewhere in the rubble of her belongings.

Finally she thought of one.

"Bebe gave it to me. She felt so bad about stealing Lacey away from me, it was her way of making amends."

"Get real, Tatiana. Since when did Bebe ever feel bad about any of the stunts she pulled? The woman was a world-class sociopath."

"Okay," she sighed, seeing I wasn't buying her story. "I took it from her studio the night of the murder. I came back to have it out with Bebe once and for all, but when I got there, she was already dead. So I grabbed the bag and ran. But I didn't kill her."

I wasn't so sure about that.

And then a most unpleasant thought occurred to me:

If Tatiana had killed once, surely she was capable of doing it again. Maybe right here, right now, in her pigsty of a bedroom. Heck, it would take them months to find my body underneath all this clutter.

"You don't believe me," she said, fire burning in her eyes. "You think I killed her."

"Of course, I believe you," I said, eager to appease her.

But she wasn't about to be appeased.

"You've got some nerve!" she shrieked, her face now an alarming shade of puce. "Coming here in your tacky elastic-waist pants and accusing me of murder!"

With veins throbbing and eyes bulging, this was one furious lady. I looked around at the many wire hangers scattered around the room and prayed one of them wouldn't soon be wrapped around my neck.

"Honestly," I said, skittering past her out into the living room, "I wasn't accusing you of anything. So why don't I just come back tomorrow for the dress," I said, grabbing my purse from the sofa, "and I'll be on my way."

"Forget it!" Tatiana shrieked. "I'm not selling you anything, you meddling bitch!"

The veins in her neck now thick as Boy Scout knots, she grabbed her monster clothing rack and—in a moment I won't soon forget—shoved it right at me.

Adrenaline flowing, I managed to dash outside in the nick of time, cringing at the sound of the heavy metal rack as it crashed into the front door.

Chapter 29

I drove home, badly shaken by my close encounter with a clothing rack.

By now, Tatiana had catapulted to the top of my suspect list—Number One with a bullet.

But I couldn't forget about my other would-be killers: Like Miles and Anna. With Bebe out of the way, they were free to pursue their race into each other's arms—and to enjoy all the money they were sure to inherit. And what about Lacey, my freckle-faced blackmail victim, who had to be breathing a lot easier with Bebe out of the way? And Heidi, who'd practically been Bebe's indentured servant, now free to work her dream job at the studio?

No, Tatiana wasn't the only one who could have wiped out Bebe—not by a long shot.

My suspect list quickly faded away, however, when I got home and found a text from Justin:

Dinner at my place tomorrow night?

Yesyesyesyesyesyes!

Call me!

His wish was my command.

Instantly I tapped his number into my phone.

"Guess what, Jaine?" he said when he answered. "I've got a new job. Personal assistant to a socialite in Holmby

Hills. Her current PA says she's a doll to work for. And the pay is great. Anyhow, I wanted to celebrate, and the first person I thought of was you."

Yay! I was tops on his list.

"Are you free for dinner tomorrow?"

I reminded myself not to sound too eager, to create an aura of sophisticated insouciance.

"You betcha! Absolutely! Sounds great!"

Aack! I'm hopeless.

"Terrific. See you at seven. I'll text you my address."

I hung up in a happy glow, thrilled at the prospect of dinner with Justin—a cozy tête-à-tête that just might lead to some after-dinner smooching and possible whoopsie doodle!

Things were definitely looking up. A date with Justin tomorrow—and a steak dinner at the Paws Across America charity gala tonight.

If you recall, the only reason I'd accepted the invitation to the gala was the promise of a thick, juicy steak on my plate.

True, I was still a bit miffed that Prozac was being hailed as the cat who saved a toddler's life when all she'd really cared about was that Chicken McNugget. But free steak dinners don't come around every day, and I wasn't about to pass this one up.

It was too bad I didn't have Tatiana's cute black spaghetti-strap number to wear. I thought about wearing one of the dresses from my makeover, but somehow they seemed tainted by the memory of Bebe.

In the end, I decided to go with my one and only Prada pantsuit. After digging it out from the back of my closet, I dusted it off, hoping no one would notice the grease stain on the elbow that years of dry cleaning had not been able to eradicate.

(A word to the wise: Never eat chimichangas in a Prada pantsuit.)

And so I showered and dressed for the gala, murder suspects a distant memory amid vivid images of Justin and a top sirloin.

"I hope you realize this is a very special day for you," I said to Pro when I was all spiffed up and ready to go.

She looked up from where she was sprawled out on the sofa.

It sure is. I broke my record for seventeen naps in an hour.

"Tonight," I reminded her, "you're getting an award for an act of bravery you don't deserve."

You're just cranky because I look fab and you've got that grease stain on your elbow.

"Time to get going," I said, hauling her cat carrier out from my hall closet, hoping for once she wouldn't give me a rough time.

I hoped in vain. The minute she saw the carrier, she was crouched on all fours, poised for battle.

You don't think I'm actually going to get in that thing, do you?

When I reached down to pick her up, all hell broke loose. Claws out, fur flying, she meowed in protest.

This is how you treat The Cat Who Saved a Toddler's Life? By locking her up in a cage? Wait till the people at Paws Across America hear about this gross miscarriage of justice!

Suffice it to say that my Prada suit now had a small rip on the lapel to go with the grease stain on my elbow.

I finally managed to lure her in the carrier with a kitty caviar treat and headed out to my Corolla.

The gala was being held at the Beverly Hilton, a posh hotel with banquet rooms the size of third world nations.

The drive over was a bit of a nightmare, what with Prozac screeching nonstop, pausing only when I tossed a caviar treat into the carrier every three and a half seconds.

Because of all the time wasted getting her into her carrier, we were late, of course.

Matilda, our liaison at Paws Across America, a tall, stork-like woman with a beaky nose and fluttering hands, was waiting for us at the entrance to the banquet room.

"Thank goodness you're here!" she said. "I was beginning to get worried."

"So sorry we're late. I had a hard time getting Prozac into her carrier. She absolutely hates being cooped up and makes the most terrible fuss."

"Really?" Matilda said. "She seems quite happy now."

I looked down and saw Prozac, the duplicitous devil, curled up in her cage, quiet as her squeaky toy mouse after she'd battered it to oblivion.

She rarely lets the real world see her inner monster. She saves that privilege for me.

"Follow me," Matilda said, leading us into the banquet room, past tables of wealthy animal lovers digging into their salads, the mouthwatering aroma of steaks to come wafting in the air.

A velvet curtain opened to the backstage area, where Matilda escorted us down a corridor.

"Here we are," she said, ushering us into a private dressing room with a vanity table and small sofa, a TV monitor mounted on the wall. "A room all to yourself. This way our little heroine won't have to be cooped up in her carrier. You can see what's happening onstage," she added, pointing to the monitor, which at that moment showed an empty stage with a lectern at the center.

"Make yourselves comfy, and I'll be back in a flash with your dinners!"

As soon as I opened the latch, Prozac bolted from the carrier, shooting me the filthiest of looks before leaping onto the vanity table and admiring herself in the mirror, thrilled with her own reflection.

I settled down on the sofa, watching the empty stage on the TV monitor and salivating at the thought of my dinner to come.

By now, I was famished.

True to her word, Matilda was back in a flash, wheeling in a food-service cart.

"I'm so very sorry," she said with an apologetic flap of her hands, "but unfortunately we've run out of steaks."

What??!

"I was able to cobble together a few steak tidbits for Prozac and brought a vegetable plate for you, Ms. Austen: Tofu ravioli with mushrooms and steamed broccolini!"

Tofu ravioli? Ugh. Somewhere out there a bugler was playing "Taps" for my taste buds.

"All our vegetarian guests say it's most delicious. I hope you'll enjoy it."

Fat chance of that. As soon as she left, I intended to grab a few steak tidbits from Prozac's bowl.

"I'll come get you when it's time for you and Prozac to go onstage," she said. "Bon appétit!"

The minute she was gone, I reached down to Prozac's bowl to grab a steak tidbit, but the little chowhound had already scarfed down every last scrap and was now industriously licking her whiskers.

My, that was tasty.

I eyed my tofu ravioli with disgust, listlessly picking at the ravioli shells and avoiding the slimy white chunks of tofu nestled inside.

(One of my major principles in life is to never eat anything that looks like bathtub caulking.)

All in all, a most unsatisfying experience.

Meanwhile, on the monitor, the keynote speaker had settled himself behind the lectern and was yakking about the wonderful work Paws Across America was doing and thanking all the animal lovers who'd shown up to fork over five hundred dollars a plate. After some chatter about spaying, neutering, and no-kill shelters, he passed the baton to a rotund fellow, a local philanthropist who'd just made a whopping two-million-dollar donation to the charity. The philanthropist rambled on about his love of all creatures great and small, until finally ceding the mic to the city councilman who'd come to give Prozac a kibble key to the city.

At which point, Matilda showed up to get us. After checking myself in the vanity mirror to make sure I didn't have any broccolini in my teeth, I scooped Prozac in my arms and followed Matilda to the stage wings, where I could see little Trevor and his mom, Trudy, were already onstage waiting for us.

The councilman, a slick guy in a designer suit and hair sprayed to perfection, introduced Prozac, the cat of the hour, and with an encouraging smile from Matilda, I ventured out onstage.

Nestled in my arms, Prozac preened as the audience applauded wildly.

Yes, I'm quite wonderful, aren't I?

"And now the moment we've all been waiting for," the councilman said. "It is indeed an honor to present this kibble key to the city to Prozac, The Cat Who Saved a Toddler's Life."

From behind his lectern, he whipped out an oversized key, welded out of kibble bits. The audience chuckled at the whimsical award.

The councilman began recapping Prozac's courage in

the face of danger, darting in front of an oncoming car to push little Trevor out of harm's way.

But Prozac wasn't paying the least bit of attention to him—or to the audience.

She only had eyes for Trevor. And, more important, what Trevor had clutched in his tiny little fist—another Chicken McNugget.

Prozac watched, eagle-eyed, as the kid nibbled on the chicken.

By now, the councilman had finished his speech and was ready to present the award.

"Here you go, Prozac," he said, waving the key in front of her face.

Prozac sniffed at it in disdain.

Sorry, pal. I only eat human food.

Then, with the agility of an eel on uppers, she wriggled out of my arms and lunged at Trevor, knocking him down to get at his chicken.

Trudy looked on, appalled.

"That cat's no hero!" she cried. "She wasn't trying to save Trevor from that car. All she wanted was his Chicken McNugget!"

The audience murmured their disapproval.

True, this was one of the more humiliating moments in my life, ranking right up there with my tush on display on the dance floor with Justin, not to mention my mortifying feud with Fun-topia's vending machine.

And yet, I couldn't help but feel elated.

At long last, everyone knew the truth about Prozac. The little rascal had been outed as the shameless chowhound she was. Maybe she'd finally get down from her high horse and stop playing the prima donna at home.

Having scarfed down the chicken, Prozac looked out at the audience, tsk-tsking their disapproval.

Hey, what's the problem? I was hungry. I hadn't eaten a thing since those steak tidbits a whole twenty-three minutes ago.

I was feeling pretty darn good about this state of affairs when the audience's tsk-tsking was suddenly interrupted by the heaving gasps of someone choking.

And not just any someone. It was the philanthropist who'd just forked over two million dollars to Paws Across America.

"Omigod!" a woman at his table cried out. "He can't breathe."

Without missing a beat, Prozac clambered down from the stage and over to the philanthropist's table, where she leaped up and hurled herself at his chest.

It wasn't exactly the Heimlich maneuver, but it worked. The offending meat came flying out of his mouth.

Now everyone was buzzing about this miraculous rescue!

No one seemed to care that Prozac was busy scarfing down the guy's steak. Instead, they all got out their cell phones, shooting videos of Prozac, The Cat Who Saved a Philanthropist's Life!

You've Got Mail

To: Jausten
From: DaddyO
Subject: Operation Secret Love

Tonight's the night I've been waiting for, Lambchop. The night The Battle-Axe is meeting The Flounder for their illicit rendezvous. And I am happy to report Operation Secret Love has been successfully launched!

This morning I drove over to The Hideaway Motel (right across the street from The Hideaway Restaurant) and put my plan into action.

I waited patiently in the parking lot until I saw the maid go into room number twelve, the room The Battle-Axe had requested for her tryst with The Flounder.

Then I made my way over to the room and strolled in the open door, where the maid was busy making the bed.

"Can I help you?" she asked.

Time to execute my brilliant plan.

"I checked out earlier this morning, and my wife seems to have lost an earring. Mind if I look around?"

"Help yourself," she said with a shrug.

I spent the next several minutes crawling around on the carpet, pretending to look for a nonexistent earring, until the maid finally left the bedroom and headed into the bathroom. The minute I heard the water running, I dashed over to the window and opened it just a bit, enough for me to pull it open later tonight and surprise the unsuspecting lovers.

Can't wait to see the look on The Battle-Axe's face when she realizes she's been caught in her love nest.

At long last, triumph will be mine!

Love 'n kisses from,
Daddy

TAMPA VISTAS GAZETTE

TAMPA VISTAS MAN ARRESTED FOR BREAKING INTO MOTEL ROOM, TERRIFYING ELDERLY COUPLE

Tampa Vistas resident Hank Austen was arrested last night for breaking into a room at The Hideaway Motel, terrifying an elderly couple, Lloyd and Eloise Pinkus, Methodist missionaries, who had come to Florida to attend a family reunion.

"My poor cousins flew all the way from Nairobi to be at our reunion, only to be scared half out of their wits by that lunatic!" said Lydia Pinkus, organizer of the reunion and president of the Tampa Vistas Homeowners Association.

"Eloise and I were in bed watching a National Geographic documentary about hyenas mating in the wild," said Mr. Pinkus, "when suddenly a man came climbing through our window, yelling something about a battle-axe and a flounder. Clearly the poor soul is unbalanced. Eloise and I will be praying for him."

Mr. Austen was arrested at the scene but later released on bail by his wife.

To: Jausten
From: Shoptillyoudrop

Just got back from bailing Daddy out of jail.
I may never speak to him again.

XOXO,
Mom

To: Jausten
From: DaddyO
Subject: In the Doghouse

Well, Lambchop. I suppose your mom has sent you the news about my arrest.

It seems I may have been a wee bit off base about The Battle-Axe having an affair. It turns out The Flounder is a party planner and was helping her arrange a family reunion. And according to your mom, the Victoria's Secret shopping bag I'd seen Lydia toting contained a gift for her niece, whose wedding shower she'd been unable to attend.

Of course, I knew none of this when I showed up at The Hideaway Motel last night and made my way to room number twelve, where I heard loud grunting and moaning sounds. I thought for sure The Battle-Axe and The Flounder were giving the mattress a workout.

So I climbed in the window, only to find an elderly couple watching two hyenas mating on the National Geographic channel.

I apologized profusely, but one of them had already called 911, and before I knew it, the police showed up, and I was taken into custody.

It was all an unfortunate misunderstanding. (I should've known from the start that no man in his right mind would get romantically involved with The Battle-Axe.)

But needless to say, I am in the doghouse with your mom.

Love 'n snuggles
(something I won't be getting from your mom anytime soon)

Daddy

Chapter 30

You'd think it'd be impossible for Prozac's ego— already the size of the Goodyear Blimp—to get any bigger, but you'd be wrong.

She clawed me awake the next morning, gazing down at me much like Louis IV must have looked down at the guy who washed his feet.

Awake, commoner! The Cat Who Saved a Philanthropist's Life wants breakfast!

"Oh, no," I moaned. "You're going to drive me crazier than ever, aren't you?"

That was my plan, yes! Now chop-chop. My food bowl isn't going to fill itself!

I dragged myself to the kitchen and slopped some minced mackerel guts into her bowl.

An utter waste of time, as I suspected it would be. She didn't even bother to sniff it, just shot me an imperious glare.

The Cat Who Saved a Philanthropist's Life wants human tuna!

I didn't have the energy to fight her, so I popped open a can of Bumble Bee's finest and watched as she inhaled it with lightning speed.

I was hoping against hope that news of last night's kitty

Heimlich maneuver would go unnoticed, but no such luck. When I retrieved the *L.A. Times* from my doorstep, I groaned in dismay to see the headline CAT SAVES PHILAN-THROPIST'S LIFE on the front page, along with that ghastly picture Sarita had taken of Prozac perched on my super-sized thighs.

Back in the kitchen, I nuked myself some coffee and a cinnamon raisin bagel, slathered as usual with butter and strawberry jam (extra jam to cope with extra stress). I'd just settled on the sofa to guzzle it down when I noticed a piece of paper had been slipped under my front door. I picked it up—only to find an itemized invoice from Trudy, who expected to be reimbursed for all the money she'd spent on gifts for Prozac—a whopping six hundred dollars!

Tossing the invoice on my dining room table with the rest of my unpaid bills, I returned to the sofa, determined to distract myself with the newspaper's crossword puzzle while I ate my breakfast. I didn't even make it past One Across when Lance came knocking at my door.

"Jaine! Let me in! I've got exciting news!"

With a sigh, I got up to open the door. Lance was sure to whip out his cell phone to show me a video of Prozac in action last night—the very last thing I wanted to see.

"Wait till you hear the news!" he cried, rushing in.

"If it's about Prozac," I said, holding out my palms in protest, "forget it."

"You mean the story about Prozac saving another life? Nah. Been there, done that. This is much more exciting."

Over on the sofa, Prozac let out an indignant meow.

Nothing is more exciting than moi!

"Guess who showed up at Neiman's yesterday?" Lance asked, helping himself to half of my CRB. "The police! They took Sven in for questioning."

"You're kidding!"

"I told you all along he was the killer. If I hadn't brought his DNA to the police, the case never would have been solved! And to think, you dismissed my brilliant detective work. You're not the only one who can solve a murder, you know."

Color me flabbergasted. Could Lance possibly be right? Was Sven the killer? Had all my snooping been a royal waste of time? And most important, was Lance about to be the hero of this particular tale?

I'm ashamed to admit, I felt the teensiest stab of jealousy.

"Well, I'm off to the spa," he said, sailing out the door. "Must get myself camera ready for all the press I'm certain to receive."

The rest of the day passed in an irritating blur.

Starting when I opened my emails and read about Daddy's raid at The Hideaway Motel. Those missionaries must have been scared half out of their wits. And poor Mom. How she puts up with Daddy's antics, I'll never know. Honestly, sometimes I think Daddy should have come with a warning from the surgeon general that "marrying this man can be hazardous to your mental health."

And as if dealing with Daddy's motel fiasco weren't enough, the phone kept ringing with calls from news outlets wanting to chat about Prozac—all of which I ignored. The sooner Pro got out of the limelight, the happier I'd be.

But the constant calls were getting on my nerves.

That is, until my phone lit up with a very intriguing text from a certain Edwin Alonzo Allbritton—who just happened to be the philanthropist whose life Prozac had saved. The text read:

Call my office ASAP.

I did as directed and got a piece of news that more than made up for the day's aggravation.

Edwin Alonzo, that delightful fellow, informed me that he was cutting me a check for fifty thousand dollars as a reward for Prozac having saved his life.

Yes, fifty thousand smackeroos!

Suddenly life was beautiful.

With 50K, I could afford to feed Pro kitty caviar forever. Heck, I could afford to feed her real caviar. And who cared if Lance solved Bebe's murder and not me? If he was right about Sven, I'd no longer be a murder suspect!

"Oh, Pro!" I cried, racing to the sofa and scooping her in my arms. "I'm fifty thousand dollars richer. All thanks to you and your monumental gluttony!"

She purred with pride.

"So what do you think I should buy with the money?"

That's easy. A fabulous new apartment. A bauble from Tiffany's. A lifetime supply of filet mignon. And something for you, too, of course.

Chapter 31

To think, a day that had started out so miserably was turning out to be one of the happiest of my life.

First my fifty-thousand-dollar windfall. And now my dinner date with Justin.

I drove over to his apartment that night, filled with naughty thoughts of Justin and his divine dimple. (Thoughts way too X-rated for your delicate ears.) Was tonight the night he'd finally do more than just kiss me? Was I about to be the grateful recipient of whoopsie doodle and fifty grand all on the same day?

If my head hadn't been so lost in the clouds, I might have noticed the car that was following me, on my tail ever since I left my duplex. If I hadn't been dawdling in la-la land, I would have been wary about parking in the dark alley behind Justin's building. And I certainly would have paid attention to the footsteps behind me as I started down the alley.

All of which is why I was completely caught off guard when I was tackled to the ground by what felt like an NFL linebacker.

But it was no football player. It was Tatiana, Queen of the Blender, now straddling my chest, her jet-black hair wild as a fright wig, her eyes burning with rage.

I tried to wrest free, but she was surprisingly strong for a woman her age, her thighs like steel vises clamping my arms to my side.

"Why'd you have to go poking your nose in other people's business?" she hissed, spittle flying. "Now you know too much."

So much for Sven being the killer. Just as I'd suspected after she'd almost mowed me down with her clothing rack, it was Tatiana.

"You're the one who killed Bebe!" I cried.

Just the mention of Bebe's name seemed to rachet up her fury.

"Bebe? The bitch deserved to die!"

So Bebe wasn't already dead when Tatiana showed up at the studio the night of the murder. She was very much alive—until Tatiana squeezed the life out of her with a wire hanger.

"If you let me go," I begged, "I swear I won't breathe a word about any of this."

"You won't breathe a word," she replied with a rather terrifying smile. "Period."

With that, she clamped her hands around my neck and started strangling me—just like she'd strangled Bebe.

I screamed for help, but my cries grew weaker as her hold on me tightened.

I was frantic now, twisting my head, trying to ease the pressure, but it was no use. Her face flushed from the effort, Tatiana's hands stayed clamped around my neck in a death grip.

"Bebe ruined my life once," she said, "and I can't let you ruin it now."

I was gasping for air, certain I was breathing my last breath, wondering if the last thing I saw before I died was going to be Tatiana's bloodshot eyes, when I became aware of someone prying Tatiana's hands from my neck.

I looked up and saw Justin—glorious, dimpled, too-young-for-me-but-I-didn't-care Justin—wrenching Tatiana away from me.

"I heard you screaming," said my cutie pie savior, pinning Tatiana up against a car, "and called 911. The police should be here any minute."

"The police?" Tatiana said. "Don't be silly. We don't need the police. I wasn't trying to kill you, Jaine, just scare you, that's all. A little horseplay between friends."

That said with a slightly maniacal laugh.

"Remember what you said about not breathing a word about Bebe's murder? Let's do that. Let's forget about all this, and I'll give you that Michael Kors cocktail dress. I'll throw in a Chanel suit, and an only slightly used Rolex for you, Justin. You can sell it all on eBay for thousands!"

By the time the cops showed up, she was offering to shower us both with free clothing for the rest of our lives.

Justin interrupted her inventory of designer togs to tell the police how he found Tatiana sitting on my chest, choking me.

"I barely touched her," Tatiana claimed. "She's still breathing, right? It's all a big misunderstanding.

"Say," she added, her eyes darting wildly between the two cops, "how'd you guys like free Armani suits? And Ferragamo shoes?"

The cops declined her generous offer and, after taking down my statement, cuffed Tatiana and carted her way.

"Where's my Birkin bag?" she kept asking, dazed, as they eased her into the patrol car.

Clearly her second stab at murder had sent her round the bend.

Chapter 32

With a protective arm around my shoulder, Justin led me up to his studio apartment.

"It's a good thing my window was open," he said, pointing to a sliding glass window at the front of the unit, "otherwise I wouldn't have heard you screaming for help."

Amen to that.

I looked around the studio, a stylish nest, surprisingly sophisticated for a twenty-year-old. But what impressed me most of all was the mouthwatering aroma of roast chicken wafting in the air.

Yummers! For a guy who'd claimed he was still trying to figure out how to nuke water, he'd done a pretty fantastic job.

His bistro dining table had been set for two, complete with candles and a bottle of wine chilling in a bucket.

In spite of my recent brush with death, I felt my heart zing.

"That scene in the alley was really scary," he said, sitting me down on his sofa and examining my neck.

"How does it look?" I asked.

"Actually, not too bad. Let me get some ice for you, just in case."

He got an ice pack from his freezer and applied it to my neck, which felt great.

Not quite as great as Justin's thigh touching mine, but still very soothing.

"I can't believe you actually tracked down Bebe's killer," he said after I filled him in on the damning details about finding Bebe's Birkin bag in Tatiana's cottage. "You're amazing."

"Not really." I tried to look modest, but secretly basked in the glow of his praise.

"I'm not surprised Tatiana's the killer. The woman has been a loose cannon for years. I guess she finally snapped. And I can understand why. Bebe totally torched her career.

"But let's forget about Bebe," he said, with a twinkle in his eye, "and concentrate on us. How about a glass of wine?"

"Excellent idea."

"I know how much you like chardonnay, so I bought some. Or, I should say, I paid some guy at the market to go in and buy some for me."

He poured us each some wine from the ice bucket and returned to join me at the sofa, my lady parts going kablooey as once again his thigh touched mine.

"Here's to catching killers!" He raised his glass in a toast.

The wine was delicious. Or maybe it just tasted so good because I was drinking it with Justin.

"I don't suppose you feel like eating after all you've been through."

Bwah hahaha! He sure didn't know me well, did he?

"I guess I could force down a bite or two," I said in the understatement of the century.

While Justin puttered in the kitchen, I took a seat at the

dining table, making a solemn vow not to inhale the meal and to absolutely, positively leave something on my plate.

"Can I help?" I asked.

"No, I'm fine," he said, bringing me a plate of glorious roast chicken, surrounded by even more glorious roasted potatoes.

It was all I could do not to swan dive into it.

I tried my best to pause between bites and not lick my fingers as Justin told me about his new job as a personal assistant to a Holmby Hills socialite. In all the drama of almost getting killed, I'd forgotten that was the reason he'd invited me over.

"She's on the board of the LA Philharmonic, so I'm hoping I can make some valuable music connections."

He gazed at a framed photo of violin virtuoso Itzhak Perlman hanging over his sofa.

"Someday I'm going to make it to Carnegie Hall."

Remembering his less-than-lackluster recital, I figured he had a long way to go, but with a glass of wine in me and Justin within kissing distance, it seemed like anything was possible.

When I'd cleaned my plate—yes, I cleaned my plate; I ate everything except the pattern—Justin reached across the table and took my hand. I only hoped it wasn't slick with chicken grease.

"I'm so happy you're here."

"Me, too."

"I have ice cream for dessert. But frankly," he said, zapping me with his dimple, "I'd rather have you."

Oh, my. Pass the smelling salts.

Then he pulled me up from the table and wrapped me in his arms.

"Let me know if I hurt your neck," he said before zeroing in for a kiss.

Neck? What neck? It seemed like centuries ago that Tatiana had been trying to strangle me.

Soon I was drowning in his kisses, feeling the electric charge of his hands exploring my body. He moved with such ease, such confidence, I felt as if our roles had been reversed, with me a giggling teenager and Justin the experienced older man.

His lips on mine, he guided me across the room until I was backed up against a wall.

"Wouldn't the sofa be more comfy?" I managed to gasp.

"Not more comfy than this."

With that, he reached up and pulled down a Murphy bed.

A bed! Dipsy doodle time!

I wish I could tell you how wonderful it was to join our bodies in ecstasy, but I can't. Because before we could even make a dent in the mattress, someone started banging on the door.

"Justin!" I heard a woman cry. "Let me in!"

"Damn," Justin whispered. "It's Estelle, my violin teacher."

I remembered the gray-haired crone with the mole on her nose.

"You've got to hide!" he said, shoving the Murphy bed back into the wall.

What? Hide? Why?

But I didn't get a chance to ask these questions because before I knew it, he'd pushed me into a closet near the front door.

"Estelle, babe," I heard him say. "Come on in."

Babe? He called his violin teacher babe?

The closet had a louvered door, and through the slats I could see him ushering in the gray-haired Aarpster.

"What's wrong?" he asked.

Peeking out, I saw her scowling.

"I'll tell you what's wrong. You haven't been returning my calls or my texts. Have you been cheating on me?"

Cheating on her? Had Justin been having an affair with a woman old enough to be his grandmother?

"Of course I'm not cheating on you, sweet cheeks," he cooed.

Sweet cheeks? Really?

"I thought I heard voices just now," she said. "A woman's voice."

"That was the TV. I just turned it off."

"What's this?"

I craned my neck and watched as she stomped over to the bistro dining table.

"Dinner for two? With lipstick on one of the wineglasses?"

Not missing a beat, Justin replied, "My Aunt Lillian stopped by for dinner tonight. I told you about Aunt Lil. The librarian in Sherman Oaks. You've got to stop being so paranoid, hon. You know how I feel about you."

With that, he reached out and wrapped her in his arms, the exact same way he'd wrapped me in his arms just minutes ago.

I was sorely tempted to march out of the closet and expose Justin for the two-timing rat that he was when I heard Mrs. Fletcher say something that kept me frozen to the spot.

"I hope you haven't forgotten, Justin," she said, breaking away from his embrace. "I lied to give you an alibi for the night of the murder, pretending you were having a violin lesson with me. I don't know where you were that night. And I don't want to know. But if I ever find out you've been cheating on me, I'm going straight to the police."

With a sinking sensation in the pit of my stomach, I realized Justin didn't have an alibi for the night of the murder. Which meant he could very well be the killer.

Was it possible Tatiana had attacked me in the alley to
keep me from blabbing about her stolen Birkin bag—and
that she had nothing to do with Bebe's murder?

"How many times do I have to tell you," Justin was saying to Estelle, the lie sliding from his lips smooth as silk,
"you're the only one I love."

Repulsed, I turned away as he started to kiss her, staring
dully at the clothing hanging in Justin's closet. And there,
in the dim light filtering in from the louvered slats, I saw
something strange. Hanging among the shirts and jeans
were two TEAM BEBE bomber jackets, one much smaller
than the other.

I sniffed at the smaller one, way too small for Justin,
and smelled a woman's perfume. I'd smelled that perfume
before. It was the same Lemon Pine-Sol scent I'd smelled
on Bebe.

What on earth was Justin doing with Bebe's jacket?

It was then that I noticed some lumps poking out at the
bottom of the jacket, just above the elastic ribbing. Something had been hidden in the lining. I shoved my hand inside the pocket and managed to poke a hole in the seam
with my fingernail.

Rooting around, I pulled out a honker ring, matching
brooch, and pair of earrings. Even in the dim light of the
closet, I could see the sparkle of many karats' worth of di-
amonds.

Suddenly I remembered the story of Bebe's family coming to America with their valuables stashed in the lining of
her mom's coat. Following that tradition, had Bebe sewn
valuable jewels into the lining of her jacket? A nest egg for

a rainy day? Had Justin found out about it and killed her to get his hands on her loot?

So rapt had I been in my discovery, I hadn't realized that Justin was finally getting rid of Mrs. Fletcher.

"See you soon, babe," I heard him saying.

As he shut the door behind her, I quickly jammed the jewels into the back pocket of my jeans.

"Sorry about that," he said, opening the closet door, a sheepish grin on his face. He flashed me his dimple, which had totally lost its power to enchant. "I hope you won't think worse of me (*was he kidding?*), but I've been sleeping with Estelle. It hasn't been fun, but I had to do it for the free violin lessons."

All along, I'd thought the old biddy had been bilking Justin out of money, when he was the one taking advantage of her.

"So what do you say we pick up where we left off?" he said, pulling me roughly into his arms. His hands, which felt so divine just a short while ago, now sent shivers of disgust down my spine.

I cringed as he groped my body, trying to break free. But he wasn't letting go.

My heart stopped as I felt his hand reaching down toward my tush and cupping the jewels I'd shoved in my jeans.

"What's this?" he said, scooping them out. "Oh, darn. I see you've found Bebe's secret stash.

"Too bad," he tsked, tossing them down on the coffee table. "And yes, I was boffing Bebe, too. I really do get off on older women. Granted, Estelle is a chore. But Bebe was much more fun.

"One night after sex, Bebe and I were doing the pillow talk thing, and she told me about the jewels she'd sewn into her TEAM BEBE jacket, in case of a financial emergency."

"So you killed her to get them."

"Clever touch, wasn't it, using the wire hanger? I thought for sure that would throw suspicion on Miles. She drove him nuts about those damn things. No one suspected me, of course. I was the one person on staff she was nice to. I made sure of that in bed.

"Anyhow, after I wrung her neck that night, I hopped up to her bedroom and stole the jacket. I figured I'd hold onto the jewels until it was safe to fence them. Then rake in the bonanza. This stuff is worth a fortune. Just think what it could do for my career. I can dump Estelle and get lessons from a real pro and become the virtuoso violinist I was meant to be."

Oh, gulp. This was one seriously deluded psychopath.

How on earth had I let myself fall for him? Why hadn't I been able to see past that damn dimple?

If he killed Bebe, surely he wouldn't hesitate to kill me. I had to get out of there—preferably not in a body bag—and convince him his secret was safe with me.

"I don't blame you," I said, forcing myself to smile. "Talent like yours can't be trampled; it has to survive at all costs. And besides, you didn't really do anything wrong. Bebe was a terrible person. You were performing a public service."

"I knew you'd understand," he said, flashing me his now loathsome dimple. "Let's pick up where we left off, shall we?"

Grabbing me by my wrist, he dragged me over to the Murphy bed and pulled it down from the wall.

For a minute, I considered playing along with him, going to bed with him, and praying he'd fall asleep so I could sneak away. But as he pressed his body against mine, I couldn't go through with it, recoiling at his touch.

"Actually," I said, "my neck is really starting to hurt. I guess I must have strained it cramped in your closet. But I do want to finish what we started," I added, forcing myself to peck him on the lips, swallowing the bile rising in my throat. "Rain check?"

I prayed his ego would let him buy the whopper of a lie I'd just told, hoping he'd believe that, like Estelle, I'd fallen under his spell, a puppet whose strings he could easily manipulate.

A flicker of doubt flashed in his eyes, but only a flicker.

Then he was smiling again.

"Of course I understand. You go home and rest. And as soon as you're better, we'll meet up on my Murphy bed."

"Sounds wonderful."

Somehow I managed not to puke.

Then I picked up my purse and headed for the door, desperate to make my escape.

I was foolish enough to I think I was going to get away with it. Until I saw Justin's reflection in the sliding glass window, coming toward me, holding up the now empty bottle of chardonnay, ready to smash in my skull.

He was going to kill me, after all.

And at that minute, I was rescued by the most unlikely of candidates—Cindy, the Jello-wrestling bimbo—and the very valuable head-butting technique I'd learned from her.

Fueled by fear and fury, I went charging at Justin, butting him in his gut with every ounce of strength in my body.

"Oof!" he cried, doubled over in pain, the wine bottle clattering to the floor.

Taking advantage of this lull in the action, I scooted out the door to freedom.

As I ran down the steps to the building's entrance, I heard Justin lumbering after me for a few seconds before crashing to the ground, undoubtedly tripping over the wine bottle I'd so thoughtfully left in his path.

"Don't bother getting up," I called back to him, "I'll see myself out."

The minute I got home, I called both 911 and Detective Washington to spill the beans about Justin. For good measure, I called Estelle at the Fletcher Music Academy and told her Justin had been cheating on her.

And so I was extremely gratified the next morning—as I sat curled up in bed in my jammies, scarfing down my CRB—to see footage of Justin's arrest on the local news. Apparently when the police showed up at his studio, they found him trying to flush Bebe's jewels down the toilet.

And Justin wasn't the only one in hot water. On page three of the *L.A. Times* was the headline SHOE SALESMAN CHARGED WITH GRAND LARCENY, about Sven Gustafson stealing designer shoes from Neiman's to sell on the black market in Oslo.

So Lance was right. Sven had been up to no good.

When he came barging into my apartment later that morning, I expected Lance to be bragging about his crime-fighting prowess.

But, no.

"Wait till you see this video!" he said, plopping down next to me and taking out his cell phone. "What an amazing cat!"

Prozac, who'd been draped across my armchair, belching Bumble Bee fumes, instantly perked up.

I know! I'm The Cat Who Saved a Philanthropist's Life!

Eagerly, she jumped on his lap to get a look at the video, then blinked in disbelief.

Hold on. That's not moi!

Indeed it wasn't.

On the screen was a brand new feline sensation—*Herman, The Cat Who Plays the Violin.*

"How delightful!" I cried, watching a tabby pluck the strings of a violin with his paw.

Prozac stared at the screen in disgust, then stalked off to claw a throw pillow to ribbons.

Hooray! Prozac had been dethroned. And she knew it. Her fifteen minutes of fame were over!

I sat back and polished off another cinnamon raisin bagel, marveling at the violin-playing cat, and thinking how much better he sounded than Justin ever did.

You've Got Mail

To: Jausten
From: Shoptillyoudrop
Subject: A Perfect Angel

Thanks heavens Lydia's missionary cousins have dropped all charges against Daddy. In fact they even held a vigil to pray for his mental health.

I swore I'd never speak to him again after that mortifying incident at The Hideaway Motel. But he's been a perfect angel, worming his way back into my good graces. Yesterday he bought me a dozen roses and a beautiful new parfait bowl. And tonight he's taking me to dinner at Le Chateaubriand, Tampa Vistas' most elegant restaurant.

What can I say? It's hard to stay mad at Daddy. I guess I love him, warts and all.

XOXO,
Mom

PS. Best of all, Daddy's agreed to go to Lydia's opera series. I just hope he doesn't take one of his "power naps" and start snoring!

To: Jausten
From: DaddyO
Subject: Out of the Doghouse

Dearest Lambchop—In a desperate attempt to appease your mom, I've agreed to go that dratted opera series.

But at least your mom's talking to me again and even made me a great Reuben sandwich for lunch.

So it looks like I'm out of the doghouse!

Love 'n hugs
(and a big sigh of relief)
from,
Daddy

To: Jausten
From: Shoptillyoudrop
Subject: Hot Gossip

Oh, my goodness. Tampa Vistas' gossip grapevine is positively sizzling with the news that Dr. Denise, the radio talk show host, is having an adulterous affair with—of all people—Lydia's party planner!

Must call Lydia and get the whole story.

XOXO,
Mom

TAMPA VISTAS GAZETTE

POPULAR TALK RADIO SHOW HOST FIRED

Popular radio psychologist Doctor Denise was fired today after explosive news surfaced about an extramarital affair she was having with party planner Lucas Grundvig.

Suspecting her husband's infidelity, Mrs. Grundvig hired a private investigator, who took photos of the adulterous couple holding hands and kissing at The Hideaway restaurant.

To: Jausten
From: DaddyO
Subject: I Was Right All Along

Hah! I was right all along, Lambchop. Maybe not about Lydia. But I knew from the minute I laid eyes on The Flounder, he was up to no good. Sure enough, he's been having an affair with Dr. Denise from the radio!

I'm tempted to tell your mother about my amazing powers of perception, but I can't risk it. Not so soon after The Hideaway Motel debacle.

But you and I know the truth.

Love 'n snuggles from your
Ever loving,
Daddy

PS. Just sent away for some military grade earplugs so I can power nap my way through those darn operas.

Epilogue

Criminal justice fans will be happy to know that Justin, my boy toy psychopath, is in jail, awaiting trial for Bebe Braddock's murder.

And it turns out I was right about Tatiana. She attacked me in the alley to keep me from blabbing about her theft of Bebe's Birkin bag, terrified it would scotch her chance at a comeback as Lacey's stylist.

Today, thanks to anger management therapy, and a hefty dose of meds, she's got her life back on track. In fact, ever since Lacey showed up at the Academy Awards in an outfit curated by Tatiana, the sixtysomething stylist's career has been skyrocketing. So much so that she sold her shack in the Valley and bought a McMansion in Brentwood, not far from Miles and Anna.

Speaking of the adulterous duo, they're now happily married and have opened an exclusive boutique, stocked with Anna's original designs—all proudly displayed on wire hangers.

In other news, Heidi's still doing hair and makeup for A-list movie stars. Last I heard, she was dating Sean, the Spectacular Studios tour guide.

Herman, The Cat Who Plays the Violin, made an appearance on the *Today* show, which irked Prozac no end. (And I've got the scratches on my TV screen to prove it.)

Every once in a while, I catch Prozac gazing wistfully out the window—either lost in memories of her internet glory—or planning an attack on the Sons of Satan (aka my new suede boots).

As for me, I sold my makeover outfits on eBay (all except that glorious blue cashmere sweater), the proceeds of which netted me just enough to pay Trudy's six-hundred-dollar bill.

And I never did get that fifty thousand dollars from Edwin Alonso Allbritton. Alas, just days after texting me, he was arrested on charges of insider trading, his assets frozen.

(So if you were thinking of hitting me up for a loan, best make other plans.)

Needless to say, after my disastrous experience with Justin, I've sworn off younger men—and dimples—forever.

For the time being, I'm sticking with my four-legged significant other. Who, at this very moment, is meowing for a belly rub. Better run before Her Royal Highness gets her paws on my cashmere sweater.

Catch you next time.

XOXO

PS. I almost forgot! Biggest news of all! Tacoma's art installation, *Planet of the Grapes*, just sold at auction for 1.4 million dollars!